# FatLand

## The Early Days

### Volume II of The FatLand Trilogy

# Frannie Zellman

PEARLSONG PRESS
NASHVILLE, TN

Pearlsong Press
P.O. Box 58065
Nashville, TN 37205
www.pearlsong.com
www.pearlsongpress.com

Book & cover design by Zelda Pudding

Trade paperback ISBN 9781597190695
Ebook ISBN 9781597190701

The song *Fashioned in the Clay,* to the tune of which the lyrics of the FatLand Anthem are set, is ©1983 Elmer Beal, Jr.

### ALSO BY FRANNIE ZELLMAN

*FatLand: A Novel* (Volume I of The FatLand Trilogy)
*Fat Poets Speak: Voices of the Fat Poets' Society* (Editor)

Library of Congress Cataloging-in-Publication Data

Zellman, Frannie, 1954–
  FatLand : the Early Days : Volume II of The FatLand Trilogy / Frannie Zellman.
    pages cm. — (The FatLand Trilogy ; Volume II)
  ISBN 978-1-59719-069-5 (trade pbk. : alk. paper) — ISBN 978-1-59719-070-1 (ebook)
  1. Overweight persons—Fiction. I. Title.
  PS3626.E38F39 2013
  813'.6—dc23
                          2013029413

To my Mom and Dad

# Introduction to

# FatLand: The Early Days

AS I WROTE FATLAND: A NOVEL (Volume I of The FatLand Trilogy), I found myself intrigued by how FatLand originated. It seemed to me that there was a lot that FatLanders simply weren't taught or weren't encouraged to question in their own history.

This was partly, of course, because almost all FatLanders were so very happy to escape from the Other Side and its horrific treatment of and discrimination against people of size that once they settled into and built peaceful lives for themselves, they were simply interested in being able to live without hate and stigma.

In *FatLand,* the first volume, we encountered the Board of FatLand and the board members' children. The members of the board fled to FatLand soon after its creation and have since made happy, contented lives for themselves.

But not everyone is flourishing. And someone who both loves and hates FatLand is determined to make things very difficult for its inhabitants.

Determined to preserve their freedom and ease of living in a place where they are accepted and welcome, FatLanders must now find stores of courage within themselves to take on the most difficult issue of all.

FRANNIE ZELLMAN

# FatLand

## 2045

THE ARCHIVES AND HISTORICAL INSTITUTE of FatLand call for recollections in the forms of songs, journals, pictures, artwork, historical and personal accounts. Our mission is to explore and make accessible to researchers any materials pertaining to the origins and early days of FatLand.

# Part I

# Angela
## Undisclosed Location
### 2045

I THOUGHT I SHOULD TALK ABOUT the origins of FatLand and the reality TV show—as they called it then—that gave rise to FatLand.

And yet what comes instantly to mind is not the TV show *Living Fat and Happy,* which helped create FatLand. I see instead their faces, as if it were yesterday—swaggering, impatient, volatile Jimmy and crafty, savvy, calculating, soberly brilliant Paul.

I miss them as I miss the sun—which is almost literal, since I don't venture out often these days.

I also promised that I would not talk about them or anything connected with the beginnings of FatLand, and was told in no uncertain terms what would happen if I did. Thirty years ago.

And I have kept my promise.

Up to now.

# FatLand

## 2045

**DASH SEN GUPTA PACED UP AND DOWN** the spartan warehouse sitting area.

"There must be something wrong," he said for the fourth time. "To bring out only five boxes representing the history of thirty-five years—it makes no sense."

"FatLand priorities were not exactly focused on historical documents during the early years," Janine Storrs reminded him.

"They had a few other things on their minds," Roberta Held agreed.

The two female archivists—one FatLand born, both FatLand bred—looked at him.

He stared them down defiantly at first, then sighed. "You don't know what it means to me to be here," he said. "To imagine that my Maya would be able to live a free and happy life here instead of being the unwilling wife of a man she does not love and who does not love her, and who ridicules her for her beautiful shape, which I would have loved and cherished."

"Even now?" Janine said. "Isn't that against the law on the Other Side now, especially after the Anti-Diet Revolution?"

"We're still about twenty years behind in the villages," Dash said. "Used to be fifty. With the advent of the Universal Electricity Outflow Scheme, all the villages are now wired. So they're getting everything you got twenty, thirty years ago. It's like seeing a star explode in space—it really happened way back in time, but you're only seeing it now because light can only travel so fast. Think of our villages as wait-

12

ing for light to travel back to them."

Hypnotized by Dash and his words, Janine fell quiet. Roberta said, "That's all well and good, but it should still be outlawed. Everywhere."

"My good woman," Dash said, "from your mouth to the ears of God."

"I am not a good woman," Roberta said.

# Angela

**IT CAME AS A SHOCK TO US ALL** when Karen Larsen, one of our FatAndProud members who worked for a cable TV network, told us that two execs loved our idea for a show—that of simply showing a group of fat people living together in a house, going about their day without worrying or making any apologies about their size.

"What will they call it?" I asked.

*"Living Fat and Happy."*

"Ha-ha-ha-ha. That's what we used to say women would be without men."

"The premise, Angie, is that this is how fat people would live without anyone telling them all day long to lose weight."

"Amen to that," I said. "But I don't understand something. Why are they suddenly approving this kind of show? It's in direct contradiction of everything most shows with fat people in them stand for."

"You're not going to like this."

"Tell me."

"They think they'll be able to pitch lots of diets and diet products and all kinds of supplements and diet centers this way."

"That's disgusting."

"I know. But it's the only way they'll go ahead with it."

I thought a few seconds. "Did they line up all the housemates?"

"Yes."

"Is there any way you or someone in your office can get hold of them?"

"They're not hiding them, Angie."

"I guess they don't feel they need to. Makes it easier."

"What do you want to do with them?"

"You'll see."

THE FIRST THING I did upon obtaining the list of prospective housemates was to make copies and hide them in certain places. Then I emailed or called everyone on the list. I explained to all that the diet and pharmaceutical companies sponsoring the show were assuming that at least a few of them would tell viewers either how disgusted they were with their bodies or would gorge themselves on the supposedly "unhealthy" snacks placed all over the house to tempt them and show watchers of the show how much "help" these poor fat losers needed to overcome their shocking and disgusting eating habits.

"Now the irony," I said, "is that I know most of us think nothing is wrong with having snacks. They're like any other food. Unless you eat nothing but these foods or eat them at every meal, there's no problem. But we've got to show the viewers, and especially those insidious Big Diet and Big Pharma people, that we are not 'addicted to snacks,' as they would put it. So what I would recommend is that you all eat good, full, tasty, nutritious meals. I don't mean you shouldn't have any snacks. Once a day—twice, if you want. And there will be 'official' snack breaks. There will be dessert after dinner, too. No one will go hungry. We've got to show these account execs who are literally banking on our self-disgust and self-dissatisfaction that we are really and honestly pleased with ourselves—the way we look, the way we think, the way we live."

The one concession we did make to the stipulations of the sponsors was that every inhabitant of the house would be weighed at the beginning of the first episode. The net execs wanted to weigh each member during each episode, but Karen and I both protested that this show was not about weight loss. It was about fat people living their lives.

Another reason I didn't mind the weighings at the beginning of the first episode was, as I said to Karen, that this way viewers could see that someone weighing X or Y or X+Y is not a monster, but a person with desires and beliefs and a life like anyone else. This way people in the house would also be setting an example by not being ashamed of themselves or their bodies. And in doing this they would be giving encouragement to fat people not only all over the USA, but throughout the world.

When the directors of the project wanted to weigh the housemates both before and after the show, Karen and I protested. We reminded them that the show was not about weight loss; it was about fat people living their lives. The compromise was that they would be weighed every other episode.

I kept wishing I could get the house members together for a face-to-face meeting before the first episode, but Karen felt it would be too risky.

We did get to set the parameters of media coverage. That was a major victory. No shorts or movies or trailers or articles about fat people were to be shown or accessed or sent during the run of the show. Housemates' visits to the nearest town twice a week could be filmed.

Everything else would be left up to the house inhabitants.

KAREN AND I HELD our collective breath during the first episode. We did make faces at the ads. It was past ludicrous for them to be showing ads for diet pills, bariatric surgery and weight loss gyms.

But we were both thrilled by the way the house members introduced themselves with warmth and humor, sometimes with irony, but never with self-loathing. Perhaps my coaching via email had instilled self-worth. Or, as Karen said, it might have caused them to hide any doubts about their bodies and appearances.

"Actually, it's quite a nice house," I said to Karen. "All these open spaces and large rooms with that amazing view. Mountains. Flowers."

"Technically we're in a valley," Karen said. "The house serves as a ski chalet in winter."

KAREN AND I HELD our breaths again through the third episode, when the definitive ratings started to come in. To our great delight, they were sky high. The viewers liked the fact that four of the eight inhabitants had become involved romantically—one of the women with one of the men, and two of the women with each other.

"The male viewers like the woman-woman couple," Karen said.

"They keep hoping they'll catch them in the middle of something. So far, though, Vesta and Kathleen have only held hands. They said maybe they'll kiss at the end."

"Well played," I said. "Give those expectant lads a tease and a thrill."

Karen looked at the sheets in front of her. "One problem, though."

"What's that?

"The house members."

We turned off a cam in the part of the house we were using for the meeting.

I CAN STILL SEE THEM in my mind's eye to this day: Vicky and Esther, Kathleen and Vesta, Marty, Ed, Dave and Jimmy—as he was then.

Dark-eyed, dark-haired Esther Sylvan, with her generous breasts and strong legs, ogled by both men and women but the love interest of Dave Mesry, of the red hair and green tiger-eyes and wide, industrious mouth. I bonded early with Dave as a good friend. He was sweet on Karen and then on Esther. He was pale and thoughtful and always insightful.

Kathleen Renson, with wide blue eyes and muscles she loved to work on when she worked out, and Vesta Meyers, of the aristocratic nose and auburn curls, who loved to paint. She painted some pictures of the house and of the housemates. I think she painted more later on, of scenes from FatLand. I was not sure at the time if that was "legal" according to the byzantine clauses of the contracts we all had to sign, but I wasn't about to discourage her. I wonder if any of those pictures are still around.

Marty Stevens, tall, blond, shambling, genial, unassuming, and secret lover of dark-haired, furry-chested Ed Gallodin, which we absolutely didn't know at the time. Well, at least I didn't. Ed did a lot of working out, too. As a group we definitely put the lie to the stereotype of sedentary couch potatoes. They were, believe it or not, California-type jocks.

Jimmy Carvie. Well. Dark chestnut hair, grey eyes that searched your soul. Against the rules to fall in love with a member of the cast of a show you were producing. But I wasn't the only one. When I would enter the house I would wave to him breezily as I pretended not to care.

I remember their smiles more than anything else.

I STARTED OFF the meeting by saying, "I must warn you that whatever we decide here, the show doesn't have long to run. So it's a question of how we want to go out."

"Why?" Vesta asked.

"Our sponsors aren't selling enough products."

"Why do you think that is?" Jimmy said, sitting with his arms around his knees on the rug, with Vesta's eyes traveling back and forth from him to the fireplace, which we lit in the evenings.

"You all look too happy."

"Would it be better if we all looked unhappy?" Vicky asked. She was knitting something, for Esther, I think.

"I guess they'd prefer us to look unhappy."

"As if we cared," Dave said.

"They're complaining that their diet ads and foods and centers and beauty aids and other products aren't moving."

"Where do they want them to move?" Ed asked.

"Into the sad and avidly eager eyes and graspingly anxious hands of their customers."

"But, man, how could anyone be sad here?" Dave said. "I love this place."

We all looked around, as if on cue seeing the house with new eyes. High ceilings with wooden beams. The Great Room, with its sturdy wooden furniture and Navajo rugs and pillows, the big old-fashioned kitchen with its long wooden table and high benches, so good for cooking and eating and talking. The fireplaces in the kitchen and Great Room. The Study Room, for privacy and sipping tasty drinks. The bedrooms with strong wooden beds, lots of space and more good handcrafted rugs. The bathrooms with wide, old-fashioned toilets,

"It has a personality," I said. "It likes us."

"Even when we argue," Vesta said, "somehow it calms us."

The front porch, with rough-hewn but comfortable chairs replete with cushions, faced a view of the mountains that yielded the most colorful sunsets and the most violent storm clouds most of us had ever seen.

"We don't want it to end," Jimmy said.

"We don't have a choice," I reminded him.

"They're not shutting us down," he said. "They're just cancelling the show."

"So how is that different?"

"We can just go on living. Right here."

"How?"

"We're already online with this. Let's tell people and make it viral. We can get other sponsors."

The housemates looked happier than I'd seen them look the entire evening.

A FEW DAYS LATER Jimmy said, "There are all these people who want to live here."

"Live where?" I asked.

"Not in this house. But nearby."

# 2045

DASH SAID, "BY COMPARING THESE SHEETS to others like them, I've found out what they are."

"We're listening," Roberta said.

"You know what television was, don't you?" Dash said.

"I have an idea."

"Basically light and sound waves sent through a charged box. Primitive, but fun at the time."

# Angela

So THERE WE WERE, WITH THOUSANDS of tents and primitive houses suddenly springing up all around different parts of the valley, and with our house now leased for 99 years.

I can still remember how the word hung in the air above us. The people in the room stood stock-still, as unbelieving as I.

"Countries need people," Vesta said.

"And land," Dave said. "Roads, other means of transport, currency, housing, police, resources, foodstuffs, industry."

"Laws," Catherine said.

"That can all be arranged," Jimmy said.

A little later, as the group had whittled down to just Jimmy and myself, he said, "You've probably heard of Winston Stark."

"What? He's the main reason we're ending the series!"

Jimmy thrummed his fingers on the Navajo rug covering part of the cool terracotta floor. "You probably shouldn't tell him that when you meet with him."

"And I'm supposed to assure him that his products will be welcomed by all when I'm trying my dammedest to have them outlawed?"

"I knew you'd understand," Jimmy said, his blue-grey eyes alight.

AND THIS, THEN, is the rather paradoxical foundation on which FatLand was built. Maybe no one is left who can put together the pieces. All of our FatLand textbooks discuss how people fleeing from anti-fat prosecution ran to FatLand in search of equality and a refuge from the Health and Diet Laws of 2014. They're not wrong, exactly; most people did come to FatLand seeking exactly those things. It is what preceded them that is never mentioned: the aborted series, the meetings, the cover-up.

On just such chances and ambiguities do the building of nation states and territories turn.

# 2045
## FatLand

OVER SMOKED SALMON, CREAM CHEESE and caper sandwiches with marinated red peppers and pickled green tomatoes on the side, served most excellently by Festal Fat Fusion Bistro at the corner of Weinstein Court and Murray Boulevard, Dash, Roberta and Janine decided on their next archival move.

"Look," Roberta said, taking a sip of wild lemon fizz tea, "our primary goal is to track the origins of FatLand. We might be able to push it ahead in another way."

"How?" Dash asked. He took a swig of Tengsa, a new and highly regarded FatLand beer. "Good stuff," he said approvingly.

Roberta said, "It's true we don't have many boxes of legacy documents and material. But the information is there in other ways. For instance, the history of occupancy of FatLand houses. The earliest ones are recorded in the Office of Deeds. We can find out who occupied the houses first and track as many as we can. Then we can talk to the inhabitants about doing interviews. Not only would this information yield some important recollections and history, but it will lead us to information about the origins of FatLand."

"The earliest occupiers would be bound to know something about the earliest times," Janine agreed. "And about their neighbors as well."

"Are you sure the Office of Deeds would have the listings from those times?" Dash asked.

"In some form or other," Roberta said. "I remember hearing that they had a couple of top flight tech people. So I'm sure they have files."

"Just as long as we remember that our primary goal is to uncover and record collections and material pertaining to the origins of Fat-Land, not just its early history," Dash warned.

"I would think that the two would be closely related," Roberta said.

"Certainly," Dash agreed. "I just don't want us to lose sight of our assignment. Sometimes if you are on the way to the top of a mountain and you enter a cozy cave, you forget that the mountain exists."

# Angela

So **THERE WE WERE, WITH THOUSANDS** of tents and small houses springing up all around different parts of the valley, with "our" house and others near it now leased for 99 years.

Winston Stark bankrolled row upon row of new houses, pushing new inhabitants to embrace his line of gyms, Complete Fitness. Admittedly at that point he did tone down the company's weight loss message, because he knew it wasn't acceptable in FatLand.

One day a young man wheeled himself over on his wheelchair. By now part of the house was the center of operations for permits and licenses needed by those who came to the valley to build houses or pitch tents.

"You've got a run on lumber," he said. "You need to start planting replacement trees now. Like yesterday." He extended a hand. "I'm Paul Winchuk."

At first Jimmy and Paul circled each other like wary male hyenas. Jimmy preened his over-the-top macho, talked about how irresistible women found him. Paul, coolly understated but intent, would cut into his exhibition with a curt simile, as in "with the discriminatory faculties of a teenage bonobo." Jimmy would respond, "Too bad you don't walk your brain a couple of times a day."

At which point I or another incensed female would say, "Jimmy, why don't you take a flying leap off one of the cliffs?" There were a few of them, about five miles away.

"He can't read a map that well," Paul would comment.

So Jimmy would stalk off in a huff until he'd cooled off.

Slowly, though, Jimmy and Paul learned to appreciate each others' abilities.

One morning I heard Paul saying to Jimmy, "You're like the Great Communicator around here."

And Jimmy said to Paul, "We'd get nowhere fast without you, my geeky friend."

A few days later Jimmy and Paul came to me and said, "Angela, we need a dining hall. And restaurants."

"And we need DSL lines," Paul added. "In addition to more wireless."

Vesta, who had come in right after them, said, "We need daycare. And schools."

"Sounds like what we need, then," I said to all of them, "is our own territory."

# 2045

"Now that we all know what we're looking at," Dash said, "let's look at more of them."

At lunchtime Roberta and Janine went outside, leaving Dash inside.

"Damn it," Roberta said. "He won't even grant me the validity of one idea."

"Men are scared of anything to do with homes or houses," Janine said. "They feel trapped."

"Too bad the first occupants of FatLand weren't hunters, then."

"Dash is a vegetarian," Janine pointed out.

"Whose idea was it to select a project leader from the Other Side?" Roberta asked.

"New policy," Janine said. "Cooperation with friendly outsiders."

# Angela

WINSTON STARK WAS NOT A HAPPY CAMPER when he found out many of us wanted to be a territory instead of a state. He was even less happy when he learned of our name/acronym: FATLAND, for Fat Acceptance Territory Lease Assigned No Date.

But Stark was never one to blurt out his doubts or show his hand. He merely said that it would make the expansion of Complete Fitness franchises a bit more challenging.

"For someone who wasn't thrilled, he took it pretty well," Jimmy observed after the meeting.

"Probably has a few things up his sleeve," Paul commented.

"What do you think he'll do?" I asked.

"Wait and see," Paul said. He looked at Jimmy, who busied himself with something or someone in the kitchen.

We didn't have long to wait. Within a month the "FreeSize Statehood Committee" was knocking on doors and getting people to sign their petitions.

"Geez," I said after reading one. "They're pretty convincing. If I didn't know better, I'd want to sign."

"I know what you mean," Karen said. "He's offering everything except angelic choirs."

"Especially to corporate establishments."

"Oh," she said. "You caught that, too."

# 2045

"You can tell by the number of takes on each sheet that the show didn't last very long," Dash explained.

"How long did it last?" Roberta asked.

"I would estimate about five weeks. If that."

"Why did it end?" Janine asked.

"It didn't end. It was cancelled."

"Fine," Roberta said. "Then why was it cancelled?"

"That," Dash said, looking two of the sheets up and down, "is what we need to find out."

FatLand Rosensteel Hotel and Convention Center was celebrating its 25th anniversary. Perks for its guests included free breakfast buffets for couples on weekend stays. The FatLand Archival and Historical Board was footing the bill for their two-night stays. Roberta and Janine stayed in one room, with Dash in an adjoining room.

That morning both Roberta and Janine were slightly hesitant to put more than a few items on their plates at first, in front of Dash, a non-FatLander. But when Roberta saw Dash piling course after course on his plate, she added several more items out of a hearty morning hunger. Janine followed suit.

"Did you both try the Belgian waffles?" Dash said as he started to eat the second helping of buffet food on his plate. "Whipped cream is out of this world."

"FatLand cows are happy cows," Roberta quoted from the current advertisement for FatLand dairy products.

"My compliments to them," Dash said. He raised his glass of apple juice. "To the FatLand cows. May they never run out of milk."

"They graze on the hills," Roberta said. "Best grass around."

That morning Roberta visited the FatLand Office of Housing Records and Deeds while Janine and Dash continued to sift through boxes of folders and papers.

# Angela

"LAND REAPPORTIONMENT CONVENTION 2014," the sign read.

"Are you excited or what?" Karen asked as we checked into the First FatLand Hotel, which had opened its doors two days before.

"All this newness, all these firsts are intoxicating," I said. "Now I know how astronauts felt when they landed on the moon."

"Free of gravity," Karen said as we stood in line to receive our Convention packets.

"That's why we have to win," I said. "We get to fly if we're a territory. But if we become a state—" The enormity of the battle grabbed and froze me.

"We won't rest," Karen said. "It'll get done somehow."

I probably shouldn't have been shocked to see people I considered friends sitting on the Statehood side of the auditorium. But—"I can't believe it," I said. "Vesta. Vicky. But Kathleen's on our side. Why did she—"

"Oh, I believe it." Paul, who had wheeled himself up to us, expertly locked his footrests.

"Why?"

"Didn't you know? I've been hired by the Convention Oversight Bureau to handle the voting."

"But Stark basically owns that!" I said, clutching the armrest on my chair.

"Basically."

"But—"

"But what?"

"You're my friend. Stark didn't mind?"

"Obviously that didn't disqualify me in Stark's eyes. Ah. Leadoff speaker."

The women's eyes rested on Jimmy as he strolled in through a side door. He grabbed the microphone and introduced himself. "We know why I'm here," he said with a big grin.

"Doesn't believe in long intros," I said.

"That's our Jimmy," Paul said.

Over my and Karen's wishes, a group from California had been brought in to oversee the Convention and physical voting, as opposed, of course, to Paul, who was in charge of the tech operations.

"How much do you think Stark is paying them?" I whispered to Kathleen, who was watching Esther, who had been appointed as a convention moderator by our own Convention Admin Committee. She introduced the five people from the California group, VoteRight, without any great enthusiasm.

"More than anyone else would," Paul whispered back as he texted.

"They're, um, not exactly FatLand dwellers," I observed, noting the collarbones sticking out of one of the women's blouses.

"You think?" Karen said, her voice heavy with derision.

I waited until the personnel from VoteRight had been introduced. Then I raised my hand. "Madame Chair."

"The Chair recognizes Angela Barton."

"Madame Chair," I said. "Whichever way we end up voting here, we are here to make what each of us considers the right choice for the governance of FatLand. It is the choice that will communicate whether people of size will finally feel easy and empowered, free and yet part of a community. Unthreatened, but looked after, acknowledged, approved.

"I wish to emphasize that we are not enemies here. Many of us can point to friends on both sides of the aisle. Many of us deal daily with and greet people who may feel differently than we do on this question. But they are all people who sincerely have the same purpose at heart that we do: to determine what we deem the fairest, the most useful, the most appropriate assignment of this land that we have already come to cherish.

"Thus it is with surprise bordering on chagrin that I note the presence of staff from VoteRight whom we FatLanders have not invited to FatLand. In direct mockery of these objectives we hold so close and so dear, I see staff from a Voting Administration Agency who, to say the least, are not holding out the golden hand of welcome to FatLanders. Do we wish to convene in the shadow of their disapproving official glances?

"Without any further ado, I propose that they be denied the right to administer this election and that another Voting Administration firm of our choice be brought in."

Amid the rush of applause and then a standing ovation, I was completely unprepared for what happened next. Two of the male personnel from VoteRight descended on me, grabbed my arms and propelled me out of the auditorium.

The sunset was almost criminally beautiful. I sat on the ground and watched as it opened into fourteen shades of rose, which tinted into lavender with edges of bronze, then dissolved into one blinding flash of red and fire.

Gone.

"Angela."

It was Karen.

"Hi."

"Come back in."

"So that bloody reich of Stark's can push me out again?"

"They're not here anymore."

"What?"

"We delegitimized and barred them from the Convention."

"Seriously?"

"Your protest and sudden removal pushed people to act. After everyone got over the shock, people began yelling and calling on Esther to have them removed. Jimmy made this wonderfully impassioned speech."

"And then what happened?"

"They took a vote. That was another good thing, by the way. Before your removal, it was pretty much split down the lines of Territorial people wanting VoteRight out and Statehood people wanting them to stay. But after you removed, it changed to 60-40."

"So Territorial people are now in the majority?"

"A lot of the unsures came over to us."

"Oh my God. Does this mean that—?"

"Just come back in."

I followed her in.

The first thing I saw on re-entering the auditorium was a banner that covered almost the entire back of the stage. It read: "Fat Acceptance Territory Lease Accession No Date" on the top half.

The bottom half read in purple, gold and green: FATLAND.

The second thing I saw—and also heard—was a roar from the already-standing Territorial voters. The crowd started to yell, "Angie! Angie!"

As it flashed into my brain that we had won territorial accession, I started to cry.

Later, when I tried to figure out where the Statehood supporters had gone, Karen told me that most of them slipped out soon after the VoteRight personnel were escorted out of the building.

"**Pleased?**" Paul asked late the next morning over brunch.

"Utterly," I said, savoring my way slowly through a cheese, tomato, pepper and mushroom omelet.

"Now the real work begins," he said.

"Paul," I said, "how did you feel when those VoteRight people were tossed out?"

"Pleased as punch."

"Hot chocolate?" I pointed to the pitcher.

"Sure."

I filled one of the stoneware mugs and set it in front of him. He lifted it to his lips, said, "Ahh," took another sip, set it down.

"Paul," I said, "you weren't working with VoteRight, then?"

"Hell, no. The Admin Committee was completely separate from VoteRight."

"How did the Admin Committee feel about what went on?"

"They split 6-4, same ratio as the rest."

I sighed. "Guess we have to try to win back the Statehood people now."

"Angie, if I were you, I'd ban them from FatLand."

"Why?"

"They're like Stark's fifth column."

"We can't ban forty percent of FatLand!"

"Too bad, that."

"Paul," I said, "if I were richer and ten years younger, would you marry me?"

"Very funny."

"Why?"

"Come on."

"Come on what?"

"Change the subject."

"Changed. Are you going to be on the Information Services Committee or the Building Committee? You have expertise in both areas."

"Both. And the Tech Admin Committee."

"At least they know talent when they see it."

"Not to mention organizational skills."

"What would we do without you?"

"Weep."

I grinned.


I **STILL HAVE** the clipping of the article that spoke of the Territorial Ceremony. In a spell of sentimentality, I kept it and put it in a folder. Here it is, word for word.

I am glad I kept it for another reason. I was afraid that Stark might try to erase evidence of the Ceremony on the smartnet. I did not even try to see if he did or not.

## FatLand incorporated as territory
### June 21, 2014

Following a Land Apportionment Convention, the Territory of FatLand was officially incorporated on the first day of summer.

A festive and excited atmosphere greeted attendees and visitors to what was formerly a part of the midsection of the state of Colorado. A band played, dignitaries spoke, banners waved.

"We are beyond proud to declare FATLAND as a Territory, and we welcome all fat people, as well as our thinner brothers and sisters, to this land of ours where people of all sizes need never fear ostracism or discrimination," the current chair of the

FatLand Board, Dave Mesry, announced.

"For two years people have been pouring into this area seeking a refuge from persecution. The outflow of emigrants has tripled since the institution of the Re-Education Centers in the USA. We needed to become a Territory to formalize our borders and provide the services that our citizens require. We hope to establish relations with all free states and countries.

"Meanwhile we now, for the first time, raise the flag of Fat-Land, our territory, our land, our home."

With these words the FatLand flag was unfurled and hoisted on a flagpole. It is purple, gold and green. The letters FATLAND are emblazoned on the bottom of the flag in gold.

Loud cheers rang out. The crowd then sang, for the very first time, the FatLand Anthem. Some were crying as they sang, but their smiles shone through their tears. People held hands as they sang and swayed.

The Constitution of FatLand, now being composed, will be read and officially declared at the end of this month.

# 2045

THEY RENDEZVOUSED FOR LUNCH AT DELHI GARDEN, which was supposed to have the best South Asian food in FatLand.

"I heard about this place," Janine said.

In the middle of the restaurant a fountain flowed and sparkled, surrounded by jasmine and jacaranda trees. "How do they do that?" Dash asked. "Do they grow them in greenhouses?"

"They used to," Roberta said. "But now the weather is mild enough, since the Climate Shift of the 2010s. The mountain still gets snow three months of the year. But the valleys get it only occasionally. They also put in artificial springs for the palms."

"Remarkable," Dash said.

"I found something rather interesting," Roberta said. They were dipping crisp Indian flatbread in different sauces as they awaited their orders—fish curry for Janine, chicken tikka for Roberta, cauliflower, potato and chickpea curry for Dash, with vegetable kofta in a dish for all. "I was looking for entries from the year 2014 and before. 2014 is when FatLand was officially founded as a territory," she explained to Dash.

"Yes," he said. "That was when the Territorial Convention took place. I read a little about it."

"I kept going down the list," she said. "There was one house that was leased in 2010."

"Who leased it?" Janine asked.

"Not a person," Roberta said. "A corporation."

"Were there any people listed at all?"

"Two years later," Roberta said. She clicked on the smartphone page. "Vesta Meyers and Kathleen Renson."

"Can we contact either of them?" Janine asked.

"Vesta is listed," Roberta said. "At that address. I'm smartmailing her now."

THE ANSWER CAME in less than ten minutes. "What is this request in regards to?"

"We have been assigned by the FatLand Archival and Historical Board to research and collect material pertaining to the origins of Fat-Land," Roberta replied. "Any recollections of this time period, especially before and up to 2014, would be of immense value to the project and for FatLand in general.

"Can you identify yourselves so I can check?" Vesta smartmailed back.

Roberta textmailed her their names.

The reply came in five minutes. "It's about time. I've been waiting for this. When would be convenient for you to come?"

# Angela

A FEW HOURS LATER, JIMMY STROLLED IN and said to Karen and me, "Guess what just happened."

"Do tell," I said.

"Stark just announced that he's going to pull the funding from all the projects he's invested in unless we rehold the Land Apportionment Convention."

"The hell he will!" I yelled.

"He can," Paul said, wheeling himself into the room.

"What can we do?" I said.

"FatLand's first Bond Drive."

"Is that cool or what?" Karen said, squeezing Paul's arm.

I looked at them in sudden understanding.

Jimmy joined me on the porch.

"You didn't know," he said.

"No."

"I wasn't sure whether to say anything."

"It's okay. I love them both."

He stood next to me, whistling. Then he touched the lowest part of my lower back.

"WELL, WELL," Karen said next morning as I came down to breakfast in my robe and slippers. "Look what the cat dragged out."

Jimmy was still asleep. I was hungry. I put a couple of instant waffles in the toaster. I was too lazy to cook.

"People were wondering where you were," Karen said.

"I was celebrating." I poured leftover hot chocolate into a cup, not caring that it was cold.

Paul wheeled into the kitchen and said, "Is he worn out or hung over?"

Karen looked at me.

I laughed. "Hot chocolate?" I said to Paul. Then I looked at Karen, who looked less than happy. "I didn't mean—" I said to Karen.

"It's okay, Ange," she said.

# 2045

"KIND OF FUN TO SEE ONE OF THESE," Roberta said. "In an eerie way."

"I don't see how it turned up here, though," Dash said, peering over her shoulder.

"That's the fun of archiving," Janine observed. "Never know what you'll find."

They all read:

### HEALTH AND DIET ADMINISTRATION
### LAW ENFORCEMENT DIVISION
### AREA NUMBER FOUR

All Area Four residents are to familiarize themselves with the following rules.

- Area Four Residents whose BMI exceeds 40 are to report to the nearest Weigh-in Center immediately.
- Area Four Residents whose BMI falls between 35 and 40 are to report to an authorized HDI clinic for evaluation.
- Area Four Residents whose BMI falls between 30 and 35 must provide evidence, when requested, to the local HDA authority that they are taking the prescribed steps to lower their BMI to 25.

"You think one of the emigres brought this with them?" Roberta said.

Janine and Dash searched through ten of the piles.

"Nothing here to identify it," Janine said.

"Not yet," Dash said.

# Angela

I PUT UP THE NOTICE AT TWO in the afternoon.

"Anyone who has seen or heard from or knows the whereabouts
of Paul Winchuk, please contact the following number or email
Karen Larsen at _____"

When I came back to the house, I went straight up to Karen's room.
Her clothes still hung in the closet, but her backpack and weekend bag
were gone.

A WEEK LATER I put up the second set of notices.
Two weeks after that, I received a call.
"Angie."
"Yes?"
"Do you know who this is?"
"Should I?"
"Indeed."
"How are you?" I asked, trying to inject some kind of normalcy into
the conversation.
"Angie, a friend of yours is sitting—no, make that standing—about
ten feet away from me."
"I have a lot of friends."
"Hello, Angie."
I sat down.

"Don't think badly of me."

"How can I judge you until I hear what happened?"

"Turn on the video."

I did.

"What do you see?"

"How?" It was the only word I could release.

"Strengthened and trained my back and leg muscles."

"In two weeks?"

"The best medical care and advice in the world."

"Congratulations."

"Angie, I fucking hate pity."

"I wasn't pitying you."

"You don't understand."

"Do try me."

"It would have been sheer torture, wondering whether or when you would have someone else."

"Paul, it wouldn't have worked that way."

"How does it work, then?"

"We could both love you, you know."

"Apparently I didn't get the memo."

"Apparently not."

"Come on, Angie. Say it. I sold my soul."

A different face replaced Paul's. "Worth every dollar, Angie, wouldn't you say?"

"Some would think so."

"You going to deny Paul his new life?"

"I deny nothing," I said.

"Charming," Stark said.

Paul was back on video. "I'm not apologizing."

"I didn't want you to."

"Bye for now, Angie."

"Bye for now, Paul."


THREE DAYS LATER, Stark called again. "I'm sorry to have to tell you this," he said. "We found your friend."

"Where?"

"On one of the mountains here."

"I see."

"Just so you know," he said, "I would have let her see him. I'm not a complete monster, you know, no matter what you think."

"Right."

"I really am sorry."

"Thanks."

I found Paul's number in my contacts and dialed. It rang. No answer.

That night I texted Stark. "Can Paul have kids?" I typed.

The response flashed on the screen in about two minutes.

"No reason why not."

# 2045

"**Why are people staring at us?**" Roberta asked. "Haven't they seen people eating lunch before?"

"Not outside," Janine reminded her. "They're still not used to that. Under HDA laws, you weren't supposed to."

"Why not?"

"It enabled thinking about food and eating."

"Oh, yes," Roberta said. "They blamed people for being obese or fat."

"Why?" Dash asked.

"So they could sell things to people. They had to make it look as if thinness was the most healthy and desirable state. So heavier people were demonized. And it became more difficult for them to get adequate healthcare. And some of them got sick or sicker or even died. But the irony was that if they lived until 65 they became healthier again, because on Medicare they couldn't be refused. If they were lucky they didn't go to doctors that often, though. Because they kept overmedicating and mismedicating them. So it was a double or triple wonder that even with all the mismanagement of their health, heavy and fat people still lived longer than thinner people. And after a while, the health agencies couldn't hide it."

"So the Health and Diet Laws were really the last gasp for Big Diet and Pharma," Dash said.

"Exactly," Janine agreed.

THE DAY of their interview, Dash said he would go over some old websites pertaining to FatAndProud, the fat acceptance and activist group in the USA which, he felt, probably had something to do with the origins of FatLand.

"Too bad you don't want to come out with us," Janine said. "It's really beautiful there. Amazing sunsets."

"Very nice," he said. "Have a good time."

"VERY WOODSY," Janine said as they drove.

"The house is in the valley," Roberta said. "The trees rise up all around it. Like a bowl."

"Did you find anything on Vesta?"

"She was some kind of county admin on the Other Side before she came to FatLand."

"Maybe she didn't want to leave."

"Maybe not."

THEY PARKED in front of the driveway, which was now extremely overgrown. "Strange," Roberta commented. "This sector is supposed to enforce lawn maintenance rules."

"Do we still want to do this?" Janine asked.

"Yes."

JANINE RANG the bell.

A woman with very pale skin, bright red hair and blue eyes extended her hand. "Good to see you," she said, moving quickly inside. Roberta and Janine followed and introduced themselves officially.

The room, a long living room, was bare except for a couch and a rug, both in Southwestern style.

"Have a seat," Vesta said, matching cream-colored top and pants sliding over her compact, chunky body, now all motion. "I'm surprised this wasn't done before."

"Now that the cold war between FatLand and the USA is over, the FatLand Board feels that it is extremely important to take stock of our own history and focus on our early days and origins. We feel that our young people, especially, need to know and understand where they came from," Roberta stated.

"The problem," Vesta said, "is that FatLand never should have been a territory in the first place."

Roberta made sure her legacy tape recorder was functioning. "Why do you feel this way?"

"Many reasons," Vesta said. "And FatLand would never have been a territory if Angela Barton hadn't pushed for it with Stark in back of her."

"I know who Stark is," Janine said. "He's the kingpin here. But who is Angela?"

# Angela

**I MET WITH MY THREE BOARD FRIENDS** that Tuesday.

Vesta, who had been completely pro-statehood and was now neutral, said, "According to all the research we've done, the main need of FatLand is people. More people."

"Even though we're struggling to house the people we have?" I asked.

"Now, yes. But soon we're going to need more."

"And that is because—?"

"Because in order to create a viable territory, we need a reliable tax base. We need children. We need a mix of people to get all kinds of work done."

"And how do you propose that we obtain these people?"

Dave, my old friend from the House who was now married, said, "By explaining to people exactly why they should come here."

"We do that all the time."

"I don't mean on the net," Dave said. "I mean in person."

**WE CALLED IT** the "Escape to FatLand" campaign.

A year after it started people would indeed have to escape to Fat-Land—often with no more than the clothes on their backs, and sometimes not even those. At this time, however, we were still an interesting novelty.

When I gave my speeches, a surprising number of thin people said they wanted to live in FatLand. They said they didn't like spending so much time worrying about their weight.

For the record, some thin people did move to FatLand.

When I'd get back from a speaking tour people would ask me how it felt, to speak on the Other Side. I told them about the Health and Diet Laws being passed and how the atmosphere on the Other Side was sick. Not enough time for all the inhabitants to get wind of them.

The linchpin, the knife in the wax, was Stark.

He called after one of my tours.

"Paul still thinks the world of you, you know," he said.

"I still think the world of him."

"He's doing very well, you know. He has his own health applications and coding firm now."

"He runs it from there?"

"Of course. And he has a gf, you know."

"Wonderful."

"Her name is Greta. She's one of his trainers."

"How many trainers does he have?"

"Three."

"Sounds as if they keep him hopping."

"He can hop now."

"That's incredible."

"Angela," Stark said, "because Paul thinks so highly of you, I'm going to offer you a deal."

"Go ahead."

"You know that the Health and Diet Laws are due to be passed sometime this year."

"And you, of course, are greasing the wheels nicely."

"Not only me, dear."

"You and others."

"Of course."

"And thus?"

"I know you've been campaigning to get people into FatLand."

"So?"

"Here's the deal. You don't campaign against the Pro-Health Laws, and I will ensure that the FatLand crossings remain open for a year after the passage of the Pro-Health and Diet Laws. So you will continue to receive refugees without too much of a problem."

"Fine, but who's to say that others might not campaign against them?"

"You let me worry about that."

"Fine."

"Yes?"

"If I find out that you've been corresponding with your FA friends—"

"Yes?"

"I'm sure you don't want to push Paul into a choice or trial of loyalties."

Paul had designed so much of FatLand's tech infrastructure.

"That would be the furthest thing from my mind," I said.

# 2045

**WHEN THEY GOT BACK TO THEIR HOTEL ROOM** Dash was there, making notes on the smarttablet. He looked annoyed. "Where were you all this time?" he grumbled. "I'm hungry."

"You have two functional hands, a functional mouth, and a very nicely functioning digestive system," Roberta said. "You are quite capable of performing the task of putting food in your hands or on utensils and bringing it to your mouth, swallowing and breaking it down into useful components, fuel and waste."

"Capricorns are always hungry," Janine said.

"I'm tempted to slap you silly with my functional hands," Dash said. "But there is so much work to be done."

"Very diligent of you," Roberta said. "Believe it or not, we seem to have uncovered a gold mine of information. Listen to this."

"I'm still hungry."

"We'll order in," Janine said.

"Then I'll miss out on the much vaunted FatLand nightlife."

"We'll dance for you," Janine said.

"Naked?"

"Maybe in another universe," Roberta said.

**THE TAPE RECORDER** played as they munched baked potatoes stuffed with cheddar cheese and broccoli and empanadas filled with chicken and beans.

"There was a convention," Vesta was saying. "It was supposed to determine whether FatLand would be a state or territory."

"Territory won, I would guess," Janine said.

"It never really got a chance," Vesta said. "Angela butted in and tried to get the agency hired to monitor the votes kicked out."

"Why?"

"She said they weren't a FatLand agency."

"They weren't?" Janine asked.

"No. But that shouldn't have mattered. They were there to manage the voting, not a dance."

"What happened then?" Roberta asked.

"Chaos. There was a lot of yelling and stomping."

"Who hired the agency?" Janine asked.

"I did."

"Did Angela know?"

"Not at first."

"What happened after the yelling and stomping?" Roberta asked.

"Some people in the auditorium started demanding a vote then and there on statehood and territorial division. A lot of other people were yelling for the agency to vacate."

"Did they vacate?" Janine asked.

"Yes. By voice vote."

"Then what happened?"

"FatLand's main info tech person cobbled together a committee to oversee the voting."

"Capable person," Roberta observed.

"Very. Angela basically drove him out of FatLand."

"Why? If he was so capable?"

"She couldn't stand having someone so intelligent around."

"How did she drive him out?" Janine asked.

"She made him fall for her. She did that to people."

"Quite the temptress," Roberta said.

"When it suited her purpose."

"WAS SHE BEAUTIFUL?" Dash asked as they listened to the recording.

Roberta put a finger to her lips.

"How did she seduce all those people?" Roberta asked Vesta.

"She was just very sure of herself verbally."

"You mean she was good at seduction?" Roberta asked.

"Her eyes looked right through you," Vesta said. "Very dark and piercing."

"How did they do the voting?" Roberta asked.

"Oh, the new committee came on stage, people started yelling "Voice vote."

"Since we are a territory, I guess the convention did end up voting for it?" Janine asked.

"I learned that they did."

"You weren't there?"

"I left after the agency I hired was relieved of its duties."

DASH ASKED Janine to stop the recorder.

"How reliable is she?"

"As reliable as anyone else who resides in FatLand and has an opinion," Janine said.

Roberta started the recorder again.

"Why did you feel that statehood was a more desirable outcome for FatLand?" Roberta asked.

"Face it," Vesta said. "We're a laugh. Thirty years, and we don't even print our own currency. Our airline isn't bad, but we don't even have the latest planes. Our markets still function mostly at the local level."

"So you feel that FatLand as a territory cannot fulfill the role of a nation without statehood?"

"Absolutely."

"But if FatLand had become a state, wouldn't it have been necessary for us the obey the Health and Diet Laws? They were the reason that so many people emigrated to FatLand in the first place."

"They might have had to give lip service, sure," Vesta said. "But there were quite a few places that weren't enforcing them."

"But why live in an atmosphere of discrimination and fear?" Janine asked. "Why should people even take the chance that Fat-Land might become like that?"

"You see that dirt path a few yard past the fence?" Vesta said. "FatLand was supposed to make that a secondary road and exit. Never happened. Why? Not a priority, they say. Now, many of us value efficiency. And speed. FatLand obviously doesn't."

"SO WHAT or who was Angela exactly?" Dash asked when they stopped the recording again.

"Answer's coming." They restarted the recording.

"How did Angela get herself into all those areas and projects?" Janine asked Vesta.

"She wanted to control as much as she could," Vesta said. "Including emigration to FatLand."

"Is that why she came to FatLand?"

"She and another person were around when we all decided to live in this house. It was the first house in FatLand. Before Fat-Land was anything."

"Who decided?" Roberta asked.

"Ten of us."

"How did you get involved?"

"My partner told me about it."

"Where is your partner?"

"We broke up after FatLand became a territory."

"Is she crying?" Dash asked.

"Yes," Roberta said.

"Why did that cause you to break up?" Janine asked.

"Kathleen was a very strong believer in territoriality," Vesta said, her voice thick and low. "Angela convinced her."

"I'm sorry," Roberta said.

"Long time," Vesta said. "But it's okay. I got my payback."

"How?" Roberta asked.

There was a muted sound of someone using a tissue. "Angela was exiled," Vesta said.

"By whom?"

"Stark."

"Since when could Stark exile anyone?" Roberta asked."He's in exile himself."

"That wouldn't keep him from doing anything," Vesta said. She laughed. "Should have seen her face when someone suggested she not run for the Board."

"Who suggested it?"

"The CEO of FatLand Free News. Margaret."

"Why did she suggest it?"

"She felt Angela was too controversial. And she didn't want Angela around for another reason."

"And that is?"

"Margaret was Stark's SO."

"Did she think that Angela would try to seduce Stark?"

"I think she was already trying."

"Is that why Stark exiled Angela?"

"Yes. She'd never admit it, though."

"You said Stark was pushing for territoriality," Roberta said. "But wouldn't statehood have benefited him a lot more? His enterprise could expand more easily. He wouldn't have to worry about different rules and borders and such."

"Oh, he made it look as if he was for statehood, certainly," Vesta said. "But what you're not taking into account is the enormous potential for anyone who wanted a piece of the action at the borders."

"What kind of action?" Roberta asked.

"Fees. The contracts for surveillance. Security. You can't have those if you don't have statehood. And let us not forget The Laurels."

"What's that?" Janine asked.

"That's where people used to go to get around the Health and Diet Laws. They served some decent stuff. Sometimes FatLand kids used to visit it as a lark."

"How did they keep open during the Health and Diet Laws?"

"Bribes. And again, Stark didn't earn most of this business because of the food."

"Then how?"

"Blackmail and extortion."

"**Charming man,**" Dash said.

"Nobody's perfect," Roberta observed.

"Something else she doesn't explain," Dash said. "Why was Angela trying to seduce Stark?"

"She admired his power?" Janine said.

"But she was friends with Margaret," Dash argued. "If they were really good friends, it doesn't make sense."

"Maybe they weren't, after a while," Roberta said.

"**There's still** something I don't quite get," Dash said after the recording finished. "The ten of them who lived in the house before FatLand was a territory. When and why did they decide? And it was leased to a media corporation before it was leased to them."

"We looked up the name of the corporation," Roberta said.

"And?"

"Nothing. Anywhere. Zip. It might as well not have existed."

"So they all joined hands and flew singing into the house? No," Dash said. "That media organization must have had something to do with it."

"She gave me the names of people who were living in the house," Roberta said.

"Excellent," Dash said. "Just treat her with kid gloves."

"Why?"

"She's on the Board. And she's still plenty angry."

"LET'S GO OUT," Dash entreated them a few minutes later. "I feel all stuffy and restless and cooped up in here."

"You just want to see those dancers," Janine teased.

"Among other things."

# Angela

"SO YOU EXPECT US JUST TO CAVE?" Vesta said.

"With Stark, you have to pick your battles," I said.

We were meeting in one of the two lounge areas in the first FatLand Elementary School.

"Why does he hate us so much?" Dave asked. He wore his usual blue flannel shirt and jeans. He looked comfortable.

"His CompleteFitness franchises aren't doing well here, even though they dumped the "diet" and "weight" from their pitches."

"He loves fat women and hates himself for loving them," Vesta said.

"Is that the case?" Kathleen asked. She and Vesta were still not back together after the argument over statehood versus territory that broke them up.

"Yes," Vesta said.

Kathleen said, "How do you know?"

"She and I went to journalism school together."

"Frankly," I said, "I don't think the USA stands a hope of reversing the Pro-Health and Diet Laws. Stark and his diet and pharma and med buddies have too much invested in them. So I figure we can play ball with Stark in this because at least the people who are threatened will be able to emigrate here without too much of a problem."

"You think all the FA and SA groups should just fold?" Vesta said.

"Come on," I said. "A lot of us came from them. They helped push for the TV series that started FatLand."

"But you think they shouldn't oppose these damned mockeries of laws!" Dave said, his angry voice belying his comfortable position on one of the lounge chairs. *At least we got the chairs right,* I thought.

"All I'm saying is that I can't be the one who meets with them on this," I said. "And I guess I'd better stop touring. And we'd better come up with policies on meetings with FA groups, on emigration and on the Pro-Health Laws."

"Not to mention Stark," Vesta said.

"That's easy," I said. "We talk to him and reveal as little as possible about what we're doing and planning."

THE NEXT DAY a very official-looking notice adorned the front door of one of the newest FatLand buildings.

*"FatLand Free News,"* it read. "Telling you everything you need to know that happens in FatLand. And then some."

A few of us stood around, gaping and gazing. I called Vesta, figuring she'd know, and that it was probably no coincidence that she'd mentioned her journalist buddy.

"Margaret Clancy," she answered. "Stark's love muffin."

"Stark's going to have a newspaper of his own right here in Fat-Land?"

"Not quite," Vesta said. "Doesn't work that way with Marge."

"You're in love with her?"

"Don't ask, don't tell, Angela."

"SO HOW does it work?" I asked Dave a little later on in the new coffee shop on Wann Way. Very exciting to see businesses and structures rising, with most of them "firsts" for FatLand.

"Vesta says Margaret's using Stark."

"Done some research," I said. "Are you sure that Vesta's not misjudging out of lust?"

"Sounds like she is using Stark," Dave said. "Maybe part of some deal."

"She gets the paper, he gets—?"

Dave grinned.

# 2045

THEY MOVED INTO MIDEAST MELANGE for baklava and the floor show, after having devoured what Janine swore were the best eggplant and mushroom cutlets on the planet in Golder's, a dairy restaurant off Winter Terrace. (FatLanders named their streets after famous and prominent FatLand poets, writers, artists, singers, sports figures and actors.)

"Heard about their floor show," Dash said. "In connection with that explosion."

"The one that killed the Egyptian dancer last year," Roberta said.

"They traced that to Stark, too," Janine said.

"Why don't they just arrest him?" Dash asked.

"He's all but impregnable in that fortress of his in the mountains," Roberta said. "When he's not flying around to different countries where his holdings and businesses are. He has his own army and fighter planes. He's like a country unto himself."

As a group of seven gloriously substantial dancers, with bellies that swirled like butter, shimmered across and strutted on stage in their fantastic costumes, Dash muttered, "We still don't know who Angela is, or why she was in the house."

"We still don't know why they decided to live in the house in the first place," Roberta said. "Now shut up and stop fighting with your urges and enjoy the show."

"Yes, ma'am," Dash said. He grabbed Janine's hand and placed it in his lap.

"I hope you're not expecting my hand to perform," Janine said.

"Don't want it for that," Dash said. "It just feels so good there."

Roberta gazed straight ahead at the stage.

When they returned to the hotel, Janine and Dash meandered in a pleasantly drunken state into Dash's room. Roberta said to them, "As long as you're not driving anywhere, good night."

As she prepared for sleep, Roberta looked at herself in the mirror. *He obviously enjoys arguing and tussling verbally with me,* she thought, *but he wants her.*

WHEN SHE awakened the next morning, it was after ten. She bounded into the shower and went through her morning routine quickly.

As she emerged from the bathroom and was starting to take a skirt and top from the smartcase, the old hotel phone rang. It had quite a harsh, loud ring compared with smartphones, she thought. She picked up the receiver, the way she'd seen her parents do it. "Hello?"

Nothing. Then a click. A dial tone resumed. Wrong number, she figured, and resumed dressing.

About half an hour later her smartphone rang. "Are you dressed?" Dash asked.

"Yes. Are you?"

"Not yet."

"Is Janine dressed?"

"Not yet."

"Are either of you planning on getting dressed?"

"Unfortunately, yes."

"Take your time."

THEY SAT on the terrace. The sun made the table glitter. There was a slight breeze.

"Might as well splurge, seeing as it's our last day," Dash said.

On a cart near them were uncovered dishes with waffles, French toast and eggs Florentine. Pitchers of hot chocolate, coffee and tea sat next to half-jars of syrup on the round balcony table.

"Glad you eat eggs, at least," Roberta observed.

"I love eggs," Dash said.

"It may be slightly unorthodox to hold a working meeting in one's jammies," Dash said. "But it is not against any law that I know of."

He clicked on a smarttablet and held it up to Roberta and Janine. "As you will see," he said, "FatAndProud reached the zenith of its membership in 2010, right before the Health and Diet Laws went into effect. There were more fat actors and actresses on TV and in movies than ever before. More cities and even states were passing statutes to end discrimination against fat people. This was at least partly due to the efforts of FatAndProud.

These advances did not sit well with diet and pharmaceutical and medical concerns who had a very large stake in making sure that fat people continued to try to lose weight. And yet—" he paused. "There must have been something that caused them to push through the Health and Diet Laws. A last straw. Something that made them feel so insecure that they had to legislate weight loss."

"How much money did they start to lose?" Janine asked.

Dash clicked a few times on the tablet. A stronger breeze blew over the table, causing Janine to cover her breasts as her robe collar flipped open. Roberta wasn't sure if it was a good or bad thing that Dash's eyes were on the tablet.

Janine said, "Whoops," and tried to tuck the robe in so the top couldn't blow or drift open.

"I saw that," Dash said. "In answer to your question, they weren't losing at all. Just adding more slowly."

"A lot more slowly?" Roberta asked, both disappointed and relieved that her own white top and tan skirt couldn't fall open anywhere in any way.

Dash clicked again. "Actually, yes."

"So that must have been the trigger, or part of it. What did FatAnd-Proud do then?"

"Some of them emigrated. Some of them started an underground effort to keep FatAndProud members and their friends and families out of the Re-Education Centers. If necessary, they smuggled them out. The Board has given permission for us to visit the main Re-Education Center today, while we wait for permission to interview someone who was the chair of FatAndProud."

# Colorado, USA
## 2045

**DASH, NOT RESTRAINABLE WHEN HE BECAME** archivally stimulated, paced up and down the empty floor. "Can you imagine?" he kept saying. "First location. This was the command center for all the Re-Education Centers."

Janine shuddered. "There should be a plaque here. To commemorate. No, to expose what was done here. For all the world to see."

"I'm surprised they haven't put one here already," Dash said.

"The Health and Diet Laws were only suspended last year," Roberta said. "Give them time."

"Yes," Janine said. "Quite a cry from suspending to exposing."

"People should know," Dash said.

"They will," Roberta said.

# Angela

**AS YOU MAY KNOW OR REMEMBER,** the Health and Diet Laws passed in 2014, as Stark said they would.

Ironically, there had been a plethora of beautiful fat women breaking into the theater, movies, modeling and even works of fiction the year before. It was as if the two worlds didn't meet or know of each other's existence—one world in which people weren't stigmatized because of what they weighed, and the other in which what one weighed was of utmost concern because low weight was equated with health in direct contradiction to the most recent research and studies. People like Stark took the utmost care to keep the two worlds apart.

At first we weren't quite sure of what the Re-Education Centers were supposed to accomplish. Their own admins weren't sure at first, either. They were provided with two contradictory sets of operational stipulations. The first was to make sure their inmates—well, their word was "clients"—were healthy. The second was to make them slim, or below the BMI cutoff of 25.

Confusion arose when they received clients who were above the BMI cutoff but whose "numbers"— cholesterol, triglycerides, blood pressure, sugar—were in the "healthy" range. There were actually quite a few fights, we learned from FatAndProud, who were monitoring the Laws and their enforcement very closely. They didn't actually plant people until the Re-Ed Centers started to focus only on weight, mostly at Stark's demand and that of the other Big Diet companies and gyms, many of whom were on the enforcement board or engaged in running the Re-Ed Centers themselves.

Our liaisons with FatAndProud told us that they felt sort of uneasy about having to become an intelligence organization, but as one FAP member put it, intelligence seemed to have deserted most of the USA. There was one point when the director of FAP said very reluctantly that they might have to sever relations with us for a while so the eager-beaver personnel employed by the Health and Diet enforcement subdivision wouldn't crack down on them. We told them that we would agree as long as one of them would meet once a month with our liaison, who would keep us informed in case some immediate action became necessary.

"What can you do?" Evie, their director at the time, asked. "Storm the centers?"

"We can work with you on escape procedures," our liaison said.

"We prefer to think of that as a last resort," Evie said.

"So do we," our liaison agreed. "But what if you need to leave in a hurry?"

About this time, right after the passage of the Health and Diet Laws, more and more families started to come to FatLand. This meant building schools, hiring teachers, figuring out what they should teach.

At first most of us thought it would be a relatively simple matter to remove objectionable and/or insulting passages from books and articles online. It wasn't long, however, before we realized that the culture of the Other Side was permeated with hatred—not only hatred of fat people, but hatred of so many who didn't fit into a very narrow definition of acceptability. It was difficult for "average" or even "slim" people to fit into their parameters and stereotypes. This seemed to hold even more strongly for women. For some reason the culture of the Other Side had ceded to a group of young not-very-intelligent males the right to judge girls and women. When had they been given these rights? We hit a blank wall.

The older ones among us tried to think back.

One of our newer board members, Anda, said, "The way I remember it, men always used to whistle at women they found attractive. When did they start to make loud comments about women they didn't like?"

Susan, a doctor by occupation and a literature buff by hobby, gave a special talk for those of us—and there were quite a few—who were interested. "The first ideas about dieting and slimness bringing health appeared in the late nineteenth century, when the Industrial Revolution was in full swing. If you read between the lines, it's as if corporate influence on the way people looked and conducted themselves started to increase dramatically then. Everyone and everything was supposed to move faster and not take pleasure in softness or even kindness. Women were now expected to be less 'there' in men's lives. Men were expected to spend less time with women because they 'distracted' men from business. Once seen as men's consciences—moral agents—women were now seen as inhibiting men's drive toward wealth and power."

"Let me guess," I said. "The supposition that we are all supposed to be within one weight range starts then, also?"

"Yes and no," she said. "Models start to get thin. But there is still some room for variation because the media still doesn't control to the extent of dominating memes.

"The CEOs who have workers on assembly lines, or drones in offices, want them to be interchangeable, as much like each other as possible. The work they are doing is deindividuated."

"So their tastes become similar," Dave observed.

"Mostly," Susan agreed. "Twiggy shape. With TV, images start to be in everyone's faces."

"Can't forget that," I said.

"And don't forget," Susan said. "The Cold War. You're in trouble if you can't roll under your desk easily. All you hear as a young girl or as a woman is 'Diet, diet. Can't be too thin or too rich.'"

When I took Susan's presentation, via smartphone, to the Education Committee, they were extremely supportive.

"That's not a bad starting point," Kathleen said. "So we show that no one body size is better. And we explain that at a later age fashions in body size helped certain people profit from the discomfort of women with 'unfashionable' bodies."

There was, however, vehement disagreement as to whether we should even use the word "diet." Some of the committee members felt that we should just tell students that on the Other Side people, especially women, are expected to starve themselves because a group of companies/corporate complexes make money from advertisements, gyms, pills, training and operations encouraging such behavior.

It was just about this time that the Health and Diet Laws were passed. The main reason given was that "obese" people cost the system too much.

Of course, when fat people came to FatLand and started to receive timely and unbigoted medical care for whatever their problems were, their "health outcomes" improved so quickly and dramatically that their mortality rates plummeted. Mostly, however, as so many Fat-Landers attested, it was living without being hated and stigmatized—and being able, simply, to walk, ride, run, swim and play without being insulted and attacked—that caused their "numbers" to improve. The first Chief Surgeons of FatLand were shocked by the dramatic and su-perfast improvement in spirits and overall wellbeing, not only of those they treated, but of those they knew—neighbors, friends, relatives.

But this still left the ticklish questions of what to teach FatLand students about the Other Side and why FatLanders decided to leave in the first place.

"Writing textbooks for us is a lot more difficult than I ever would have believed," Margaret Clancy said at one of the meetings. "It's not only what gets said, but what doesn't get said."

At first we were hesitant to make her a member of any of the com-mittees, but she wrote very well, was extremely articulate, and pub-lished our proceedings in her newspaper and online. Our deliberations and decisions were being published for now only in FatLand sites and pages and blogs, but were available to anyone who wished to access our sites. Since the passage of the Health and Diet Laws, however, a lot of our sites were now blocked by authorities on the Other Side. Stark, we figured. All the more reason to treat Margaret well, we thought.

But Margaret was as strongly critical of Stark as we were. "The SOB funds my newspaper," she declared to a few of us as we hoisted a few excellent dark beers at the first FatLand Tavern. "It doesn't mean I have to like him."

"I know exactly what you mean," I said to her a little later. "About teaching materials. We have to rewrite so much. Not because most of the facts and dates are different, but because of the emphasis and what present and recent texts from the Other Side just assume."

"Like whether people are thin or heavy?"

"It's worse than that. They assume that everyone should be and should want to be what they call 'fit,' for which read 'thin.' They write of trimming 'needless fat' off meat, budgets, schedules. In my view, those three things are much better off with some fat, so to speak. It's an entire mindset. 'Firm' versus 'soft,' 'fast' versus 'slow,' 'productive' versus 'dreamy.'"

"The corporate mentality and view of physicality."

"Exactly," I agreed.

In those days, what with the Health and Diet Laws and the borders between us and the Other Side being kept tenuously open, we judged it best that our founding meme—the one that would go into the textbooks—not sound combative or heroic. I still believe we were right about the first. I now feel we were dead wrong about the second.

Be that as it may, our statement of purpose was as follows:

> People come in all shapes and sizes naturally. It is better to live among people who respect your mind and your body. This is why people come to FatLand.
> We totally refuse the approach of the USA and the Health and Diet Laws, and the Re-Education Centers that monitor citizens' weights.
> It is better to live among people who respect not only your mind, but your body, whatever size it is, and do not ask you to change its shape.

And we put the following into our textbooks:

> People used to believe that everyone was supposed to be close to the same size, even though there are lots of different kinds of people with many different body shapes. When the Health and Diet Laws were passed in 2011 the USA set up places called Re-Education Centers, where they starved fat people in order to get them to lose weight. But many didn't lose weight at all. Those who did gained it back over the next year, even when they hardly ate. The Fat Liberation group FatAndProud smuggled out as many as they could.

None of us wanted to discuss the TV show. Stark offered to underwrite our textbooks if we didn't mention the show. What Stark didn't realize is that we probably wouldn't have wanted to put it in our textbooks even if he hadn't threatened to cut off funding for the *FatLand Free Press.*

At first I used to wonder if Stark had a conscience. Later I realized that mentioning Stark and conscience in the same breath was more than an anomaly or a dissonance; it was a complete disconnect. Stark had no conscience, probably hadn't ever had one, would find the word unreal, flat, sound signifying nothing. In Stark's universe people crafted pseudo-feelings according to their business needs. Control was assumed. Complete information was complete power.

"Publish and be damned." We would have liked to say the words to him, but we wouldn't have been able to make use of his funds.

So we bit the bullet. And instead of chaos we had textbooks paid for, schools which were not fire traps and an infrastructure carefully built and maintained.

"They will ask questions, you know," I texted Stark. "Especially the older kids."

"Just tell them that besides publishing health and science, we publish social science and manufacturing journals."

"How humanitarian of you."

"We are."

"In whose universe?"

"In all the universes you'll ever know, Angela."

# 2045
## California, USA
# Recreation Day

ROBERTA SAID, "DASH, YOU MAY KNOW that on the Other Side, during the Health and Diet Laws period, they basically starved people who had the misfortune to be sent to the Re-Education Centers."

"And what if that didn't work?" Dash asked.

Janine said, "They starved to death."

"I think I need a drink," Roberta said.

"I think we all do," Dash agreed.

THE CAVERN BAR, not far from the ocean, greeted them.

"We've only been open a month," the man who welcomed them at the doorway said. "That's when we got the okay, after—" He stopped. "After the petition went through. But to tell the truth, I think they wanted to put it through as fast as possible. They lost revenue like anything during the—" He stopped again. "During that time."

"Please excuse us for noticing," Dash said, "but you refer to the Health and Diet period as 'that time.' Are you not allowed to mention it, even now?"

The man, who seemed to be some kind of manager, said, "Come inside."

They followed him in. He gestured to a table, waited until they were seated, then sat down next to Roberta. Dash sat next to Janine and across from Roberta.

"You asked an interesting question," the manager said. "I'm Dell, by the way." He shook hands with all of them. "I guess there's no real reason why I can't mention the name, since those laws have been repealed. They were voided in this state before that, anyway. We were keeping up with everything that was happening and hoping like hell they'd repeal. Kept on thinking of Prohibition more than a hundred years ago, but this was so much worse. Even then, if you were drunk and went to jail you got out in a few days with some embarrassment, but pretty minor grief. They didn't kill you over it. No, strike that. The worst part was getting people to say in front of everyone that they were worthless to society unless they lost weight. A lot of people here will never forget or forgive that."

"Thanks for telling us," Janine said. "I guess you know we're from FatLand?"

"Kind of figured," Dell said. "Mostly because you didn't seem scared."

"Are a lot of people still scared, then?" Dash asked.

"They're still afraid that the Laws'll come back in some form or other," Dell said. "Even though the continental authorities keep putting out bulletins that restaurants are now open and bistros are back and bars are humming. People are scared they'll be seen going to them. Did you know they used to have cams all over the place?" He looked around. "For goodness sake," he said, "here you are in my bar and I haven't even asked you what you want to drink."

"Screwdriver for me," Roberta said.

"Bloody Mary," Janine said.

"What kind of beer do you have on tap?" Dash asked.

# Angela

**STARK DID KEEP HIS WORD** on letting the FatLand borders stay open for the first two years of the Health and Diet Laws.

The first inkling that policy had changed reached us just as the Fat-Land Board was in the process of apportioning revenue for schools, roads, public transit, clinics, hospitals, small businesses, adult recreation, child recreation and a few other areas. The apportionment took place every six months. The headline in the *FatLand Free News*—obtainable on paper and online—read: *Americans stopped from leaving the US at American side of border with FatLand.*

Dave, who had been reelected to the board six months ago, said, "I didn't see this coming. They were pretty cooperative up to now. Why the abrupt switch?"

The next day I emailed him. He replied, "I guess the quotient of goodwill has been exhausted."

**WE ARRANGED** a meeting with Stark. It was held just on the Other Side in a place called The Laurels. Margaret, who was with me for the meeting, asked me if I had ever heard of The Laurels.

"No. Tell me."

"It's where everyone goes when they want to eat real food."

"But how can it keep existing?"

"They get around the law by paying more taxes. People say they get breaks for serving free meals to certain people. In any case, that's not what you should be worrying about."

"What should I be worrying about?"

"Let's meet for drinks tomorrow. My treat."

We met at the newly and crisply appointed Soeur de ma Soeur on Bacon Street, named after one of the foremost health/fat acceptance researchers of the early 21st century. We sat at the counter because Margaret liked pretzels with her beer.

"Thanks for helping me with this," I said. I ordered my usual Vodka Collins.

"I don't want Stark to get his paws on you," Margaret said. "Want some pretzels?" She took a handful.

"Stella Artois," I said as she took a long sip. "Very nice."

"Might as well," she said. "After all those years of starving."

"You know something?" I said. "You just reminded me again of what we still fight. Thanks."

"That wasn't sarcastic, was it?" she said, grabbing another handful of pretzels.

"Certainly not."

"Well, then." She dusted her hands with a napkin. "Have you been keeping up with border crossing changes?"

"They're not letting people in most of the time now."

"Do you know why?"

"No."

"You have to bribe the guards now."

"That's kind of weird," I said. "I mean, if Stark wanted the borders closed or de facto closed, why didn't he just request it?"

Margaret said, "It's even weirder than you think."

"Tell me."

"He gets off seeing FatLanders bribe the guards."

"How does he know who bribes whom?"

"He's a big fan of cams."

"I thought he was just evil and rapacious. I didn't know he was sleazy."

We both laughed. "So how do we go about bribing guards?" I asked.

A FEW DAYS LATER we drove slowly to the Central checkpoint.

At the last report, Margaret told me, there was still not too much of a problem with this checkpoint. "I hope it hasn't changed too much," she added.

"You do the smiling," I said. "I tend to glower."

"Oh, come on," Margaret said as we passed hills wreathed in snow. At any other time they would have held me spellbound. "You gave all those speeches. I doubt that you glowered then."

"I did," I said. "At times."

"And when they wanted your autograph?"

"Occasionally."

Suddenly the first signs appeared. "Exit for Central FatLand checkpoint. Please proceed with extreme caution."

"They don't shoot over the border, do they?" I said.

"Not that I've heard."

Margaret stopped about twenty feet from the checkpoint. "Okay," she said. "Let's go over it one more time. There's usually a lot less trouble getting over to the US than getting back to this side. They will ask us why we want to visit the US. We will say 'business meeting.'"

"You don't think Stark will try to pull anything before the meeting?"

"He has no reason to do so."

We passed easily, albeit reluctantly, through the FatLand side. I knew one of the security people somewhat. She sighed on hearing where we were going.

"We get different reports." She looked at Margaret. "I see you've been to the US a few times this year."

"Business for my news agency," Margaret said.

The security person returned our passports. "As part of our job," she said, "we advise our FatLand citizens about what to do and where to go if they encounter problems. Since the US has not formally recognized us, we have no embassy or consulate offices. We are, however, represented from one of the Swiss missions. It is located in Madison, Wisconsin. If you were going further, I would advise you to check in with them. But since you are only going just over the border, I must tell you to pick up a few pies or boxes of cookies or cakes and have them ready on the way back. That shouldn't be difficult, anyway, since you're going to the place a lot of people buy them from."

"Quite right," Margaret agreed.

"I know you've done this before," Lucille, the security person, said.

"A few times."

She stamped our passports with exit permits which would also let us back into FatLand without any lengthy questions or searches. "Good luck. Be careful."

"Thanks," I said, my heart starting to thud.

Margaret stopped the car once again before we came to the US checkpoint.

"Ready?" she asked.

"I guess so."

There was a long and wide iron gate with four guards in black uniforms. "It feels like we're invading Mordor," I said.

"With orcs," Margaret said.

The sign read: "US–FatLand Central Checkpoint. Please have your passport and visa papers ready for inspection."

"Good afternoon," one of the guards said. "Passport and papers, please."

Margaret handed him her passport and visa. He looked at them, then handed them to one of the other guards, who looked at them in turn.

"Looks okay," the second guard said. "Take it inside and have it stamped."

I handed my passport and visa to the first guard.

As he kept looking at the picture and the entries, I grew somewhat uneasy.

Not giving back the passport, the guard said, "Would you step this way, please?"

I followed him into a long, low, grayish green building. As per Margaret's instructions, I didn't ask questions.

"JC," the guard said to someone sitting at a desk with his back to us, "This one has multiple stamps. In and out a lot."

The man sitting at the desk turned around.

My eyes fastened in unmasked shock on Jimmy.

# 2045

"MY MOM USED TO SCARE US WITH STORIES about the Other Side," Roberta said. She held up an expired passport from one of the boxes.

"About the Other Side or getting to the Other Side?" Janine asked. She held up an Advisory Sheet dated January 12, 2015.

To All FatLand Residents:

It has come to our attention that FatLanders attempting to cross back into the US at the Southern Checkpoint have experienced uncomfortable and at times harrowing situations involving guards and other security personnel. We therefore advise against using this checkpoint in the future.

"That's interesting," Dash said. "They didn't want them in the USA and yet they didn't want to let them go back to FatLand."

"They don't mention other checkpoints," Janine noted.

Roberta rifled quickly through the papers in the same bunch. "Nope," she said. "No mention of the other checkpoints."

"When did your mom scare you about the Other Side?" Dash asked.

"She said some FatLand guards used to harass FatLand women. She said it was even worse, at times."

"At least they don't do that anymore," Janine said.

# Angela
## 2015

JIMMY LOOKED AT ME AND SAID TO THE OTHER MEN standing and sitting nearby, "You can go."

The two men looked at him, then at each other, jabbed each other in the ribs, grinned, and walked out.

"Ms. Barton," he said, "we are required by law to advise you that anything you say may be held against you. If you wish to have a lawyer present, we will grant you that right, but it will delay your trip."

"What do you wish to ask me?" I said, trying to remain calm as Margaret and I had discussed.

He said, "Come with me." He took my arm and steered me into one of the rooms in the back. An examination table took up the middle of the room. There were two plastic chairs on either side.

He closed the door behind us and locked it.

"Jimmy," I said.

"Take off your clothes."

"Excuse me?"

"I said, "take off your clothes.""

"And if I won't?"

"I'll take them off for you."

"I want it recorded," I said, "that I do this under protest."

"Fine," he said.

"Is this really necessary?"

He looked at me slowly, starting with my chest, going all the way down to my feet, then traveling up again. "Very," he said, standing up and pressing his mouth against mine.

"You know," I said a little later, "no one knew where you were."

"Angie," he said. Then he lifted his left underarm.

"Umm, lovely pits, but—oh."

A very small circle, yin-yang, in purple, gold and green. The FatLand flag marker.

FatLand Intelligence Network.

He put his hand on my mouth and shook his head.

I nodded. He took his hand away.

"I never stopped wanting you," he said.


THE DILEMMA in which I had now been placed hit with full force when I rejoined Margaret, who had been waiting in the bare, drab checkpoint holding room.

Margaret seemed to be very much on the side of FatLand in all things, and her paper, the *FatLand Free News,* never failed to come down very hard on Stark and all other people and companies trying to undermine or destroy FatLand. Yet she was still taking money from him.

"I was pretty worried," she said.

"I think I'm okay."

"We won't talk about it here. Wait till we're on the road."


AS WE DROVE toward The Laurels, another thought occurred. If Margaret did somehow know about Jimmy, then my not telling her would seem highly suspect.

The Laurels were about a ten-minute drive from the Central Checkpoint. I was sure that we weren't the only FatLanders to meet with Americans there. Not only was it the most convenient meeting place for miles, but it also boasted the best—some would say the only—"real" food in the entire midwestern USA.

Margaret parked, then clicked the engine off.

So quiet. Everything seemed muted.

"Wouldn't you figure there'd be a few cams in this place?"

"Of course there are," Margaret said. "Stark owns it. He figures that sooner or later, almost everyone will come here."

"But why would he push what is essentially an anti-food system and own a very non-compliant restaurant?"

"He gets to hold it up to anyone who's been here. So they have to go along with whatever he asks."

"Right. Guess we might as well get it over with."

"Angela, you know that the checkpoint agents also report to Stark, don't you?"

"Hmm. Well, he only asked me why we were going to the USA. And in a little more detail."

"For over an hour?"

"Also how much money we were carrying, how long we intended to be here, why I had so many entries on my passport. He went over each one pretty thoroughly."

"Did you tell him why you were here before?"

"Yes. I kept wondering if they'd keep me. I mean, it must be some kind of crime to try to convince people to come to FatLand."

"It is."

"Then I guess I was lucky."

I decided not to tell Margaret that my breasts still tingled and ached. Nor, and especially not, about the FatLand marker under Jimmy's left arm.

We got out.

"The best way to proceed," I said, "is to state what we want. Simply. We're only asking for another two years."

Margaret said, "You don't know him very well, do you?"

"Why?"

"He likes to feel that he's won something every time."

"Oh. Then we'd better say we want five years."

"Yes. That's more like it."

Stark stood up as we entered. I tended to forget how ordinary he looked—a pale dark-haired man, in a business suit and tie, without any distinguishing physical characteristics. "Ladies." He bowed his head slightly, then sat back down.

I nodded. Margaret just sat down.

"What will you have?" he asked.

"Chicken pot pie," I said. "Iced tea with lemon."

"Broiled sole almandine," Margaret said. "With rice pilaf. Coffee with cream, no sugar."

If he expected us as Fatlanders to gorge, he must have been disappointed. He held a glass of some kind of juice.

"Thank you for joining me," Stark said as we finished our main courses. "They have some wonderful desserts."

"Which most USA citizens are not allowed to enjoy," I pointed out.

He stared at me. "That is simply not the case. If you maintain your weight and your health profile numbers, of course you can enjoy them. Just not every day."

"Sure," I said. "And if they can afford them, with the Health Tax. Most can't."

He said with every appearance of patience, "They can. Again, just not every day."

I wanted to knock his head to the floor and yell, "And who the hell are you to tell them or to have others tell them what they can and can't enjoy, and when? Who are you to make others medicalize food so much that it becomes a collection of chemicals and calories that make food an instant enemy if they even think of enjoying it?"

But we were here for a very different purpose, one which would not be furthered or achieved for FatLand if I gave into my desires to toss him into the nearest river.

Margaret, on the other hand, remained calm. She was probably used to dealing with him.

"We thought it would be a good idea to straighten out border requirements and procedures," she said. "For visiting and emigration."

Stark nodded. "The policy at this point, I would say, is that there will be visitation, but no emigration from the USA to FatLand."

"I take it there will also be no emigration from FatLand to the USA," I said. "But will there be visitation?"

"On limited visas," Stark said.

"One month and three months?" I asked.

"Two months."

I said, "How will FatLanders be treated during the time they are in the USA? Will they be subject to your Health and Diet Laws?"

"As long as they don't make a cheesecake run every night, I don't think they'll have to worry. Just make sure they have their paperwork on them at all times."

"That is unworthy of you," I said. "Most FatLanders don't eat much cheesecake. Secondly, we have it from reliable sources that people who are over the BMI of 30, and some who are over the BMI of 25, are being forced into Re-Education Centers. What do you have to say to that?"

He looked at Margaret and said, "Tell your friend here that she better make sure to keep her nose very clean when she comes to the USA." Then he stood up and walked out.

"I don't plan on going to the USA again," I called after him. "Ever."

Margaret said, "We had better get out of here. And we can't take the same checkpoint."

As we made our exit from The Laurels, I said, "Look at those people. I feel so bad for them."

"So do I," she said. The diners we now saw through the windows were eating very quickly, not looking up, as if they were afraid that the food would be taken from them. And they were paying through their noses for it.

"You know what he's going to do, don't you?" Margaret said as we drove toward the Northern Checkpoint.

"About emigration?"

"Yes. Anyone who attempts to emigrate to FatLand by car will be stopped and sent to a Center unless FatLand makes a specific request. And even then he'll play with the board and ask for more concessions."

"What about visas?" I asked, looking back as we drove, expecting to see and hear a car gaining on us. But it remained quiet. There was no moon that night.

"He'll let them grant a few, but he'll have them harassed."

"Even businesspeople?"

"Especially businesspeople."

We came to the Northern Checkpoint in half an hour.

"I wish it weren't so late," I said. "But better to get it over with than stay in the USA, even for a night."

"We both have friends here," Margaret said. "They wouldn't let them get at us."

"But then we'd be putting our friends in danger."

"They're probably in danger already," Margaret pointed out. "We both have pretty outspoken friends."

It was very quiet at the Northern Checkpoint. We breezed in, breezed out.

"What the hell," I said as we walked as quickly as we could toward Margaret's car. "I heard all sorts of bad things about this checkpoint."

"Maybe someone was just transferred, and there wasn't anyone around to impress by giving us a hard time," Margaret said.

"Very narrow window," I observed.

A minute or so later when we saw the sign for the FatLand border, I almost cried in relief.

The two guards on duty, Elana and Jarris, took one look at our faces and motioned us both to sit down in the trailer. We sank into the spacious FatLand chairs.

Elana handed us both mugs and pointed to pitchers of hot chocolate and coffee on the tray near our chairs. "Relax," she said. "If you can."

Margaret laughed. "*The FatLand Free News* will be running the story."

Jarris laughed in turn. "Was it really bad?"

I looked at Margaret. We couldn't mention Stark. And we certainly couldn't say anything about Jimmy.

"Let's just say it was like waiting for thunder to fall," Margaret said. "We avoided the worst by this much."

"Sounds like back and forth travel is going to be a thing of the past," Jarris said.

"That is how it is now," Margaret agreed.

"This may sound like an absurd suggestion," Elana said. "But do you think you would like to avail yourself of Safe House accommodations for the night?"

I expected Margaret to pooh-pooh the suggestion politely, considering that we both had places of our own in FatLand. Instead she said, "I don't think it's absurd at all. Angie," she looked at me, "I think it might be a good idea."

I caught the pressure in her tone. "Sure," I said. "Let's do that."

We filled out a few pages worth of paperwork. Then Jarris handed us both keys. "Number 37," he said. "Straight through the trees on the right side. Pull the car up to the parking lot at the end of this lane, then walk the rest of the way. You'll find kitchenware and utensils and towels and linen in the closets near the door."

He then added, "There's probably no cause for alarm, but don't walk around outside until after sunrise tomorrow."

"We won't," Margaret assured him. "Thanks so much for all your help."

# 2045

## California—Pacific Ocean

"IT JUST GOES ON AND ON," Roberta said.

"That's what oceans do," Dash agreed. "I lived near one for a time. That's why I wanted to see this one on our vacation day."

"Lucky you," Janine said. She tossed off her clothes, walked quickly into the water and swam away.

Roberta gazed after her. "Oh, well," she said, and sat down on the blanket in her dark blue one piece.

Dash, clad in a black boxer-type suit, ran into the ocean and swam out to where Janine was diving, swooping and working her legs. As she surfaced to tread water, Dash grabbed her around the waist from behind.

"Eeeek!" she yelled, and turned. Dash grabbed her again, held her to him and kissed her hard and thoroughly on her mouth. Her full, somewhat tan breasts pushed against his chest hard as she kissed him in turn.

Yanking off his suit, he encircled her waist and gentle curves of stomach as he fingered and pushed into soft wetness, much wetter all around now. He replaced his finger with his larger, thicker and now hard organ.

Janine rode him easily in the ocean, which every once in a while sent a large, powerful wave to shore. When they had satisfactorily exhausted themselves, they swam slowly to shore.

"I want to sleep for two weeks," Janine said.

"I want to sleep in you," Dash said.

Roberta stood up, shook out her blanket, folded it, and walked ahead of them back to the hotel.

When they returned, they found the following communication on their tablets: *Interview arranged. Must be carried out according to the following rules.*

# Part II

# Angela

**As you can imagine, the next day** we called a board meeting.

"What do you propose?" Vesta, now chair, asked me after I informed the board about our trip to The Laurels and back.

"I think we can kiss any idea of normal immigration or emigration goodbye. I believe that the best idea for the present is to concentrate more on innovations for our own infrastructure, utilities and facilities."

**From the minutes** of the FatLand Board meeting May 7, 2015:

> It was agreed that FatLand must now think of itself and build up its own strength as an independent national entity with its own needs and identity. According to the agreement, the USA will not try to send immigrants to FatLand, and FatLand will not try to send immigrants to the USA. Short stays in either country for business purposes will be tolerated, but not encouraged. Fat-Landers who keep a low profile in the USA and do not overtly challenge or protest against the Health and Diet Laws will not be subject to arrest or detention. The USA has officially forbidden emigration to FatLand.
>
> It was agreed that we shall adopt the following policy toward illegal emigration from the USA: If an emigré makes herself or himself known to a FatLander and evinces solidarity with the principles of FatLand as set forth in the FatLand Declaration of Independent Territoriality, as well as a wish to become a legal and lawful citizen of FatLand, she or he shall be encouraged to reside in FatLand and shall be eligible for citizenship ten years after date

of emigration from the USA.

Thus far the U.K. and Australia have contacted FatLand regarding immigration issues and relations with FatLand. We have met with emissaries of each nation who have stated that they consider FatLand a national entity, and while not worthy of consulate status, have set up missions in FatLand. Accordingly their nationals shall be granted rights given to diplomats residing in friendly countries.

So, in effect, for the time being, the borders of the USA were sealed off for all but short business trips. Time, then, to concentrate on our own issues and growing our identity.

THE MINUTES of the next board meeting mentioned four areas uppermost in the minds of most FatLanders: the mondo-sized FatLanders (over 500 now), FatLanders recovering from weight loss surgery, FatLanders recovering from eating disorders, and possibly the most frightening, FatLanders recovering from anti-food hypnosis.

As you can imagine, good medical care for FatLanders was a priority from the very beginning of the Territory. To start with, people emigrating from the USA to FatLand had low self-esteem and years of (failed) dieting that often rendered their metabolisms almost nonexistent and caused them to lose muscle, not fat.

The first action by FatLand's Medical Board was to institute a series of measures to introduce strength training. This was adjudged to be useful across the board for the mondo-size, post-diet, eating-disordered and low-esteem categories and one other group I will discuss later. We figured that not only would strength training help people from these groups feel stronger and more in control, but would also give them a purpose and a grid of goals to meet.

Where once upon a time post-diet and eating-disordered people had counted calories and at times taken masochistic pleasure in denying themselves tasty foods, now, if they wished, they could set training goals of doing a particular exercise or set of exercises a certain number of times a day, a week, a month. We gave them options depending on their personalities and personal histories: intense—five hours in training; moderate—two or three hours per day; light—which meant half an hour to one hour; and none.

All categories also carried the option of discussing their feelings about exercise or anything else with a counselor. Trainees also selected the amount of counseling they wanted in hours per week. They could change their options at any time, as could those who initially didn't wish to be counseled at all.

Trainees could also choose the kind of training group in which they wished to participate: large class, smaller workshop, alone but accompanied, alone without trainer assistance.

The overwhelming number of trainees were happy with their programs and thrilled with the results. The ones that made me cry were the mondo-sized in wheelchairs who had been told on the Other Side that they would never walk again. In nine months' time ten of them were walking; twelve were swimming. Their so-called numbers—measure of blood pressure and blood sugar (FatLand medical staff found cholesterol measurements useless)—improved as well. But most dramatic was the way they actually started to take an interest in their surroundings and their lives again. They started to ask for favorite foods instead of eating what they were given; they started to participate in FatLand activities, which took in anything from skydiving to skiing to Chinese checkers to gaming.

Our medical personnel attributed what seemed like miraculous improvement by many to the strong and compassionate counseling program. It was only a little later that they were able to include the simple lack of stigma in helping mondo-sized wheelchair-bound trainees to become mobile and interested in their lives once more. One of them said the following in a FatLand medical journal: "When you ride or walk out your door and everyone treats you naturally, with simple courtesy, and assumes you have as much of a right to be in a place as anyone else—after having been denied this right for so many years and having been teased, insulted and even physically assaulted—it is as if you've been transplanted to another world and given a new lease on life. It's as if you've been granted wings."

Sometimes I wondered how Paul would have responded to FatLand muscle training, had he been left in FatLand instead of being spirited off by Stark. I could imagine his blondish Norwegian Minnesotan face in front of me, laughing derisively. "Angela, you wouldn't give me a straight answer when I asked you if you were attracted to me, and here you want me to answer even more personal questions?"

And I could imagine myself looking straight into those Viking-bright berserker-blue eyes of his and saying, "Yes, I do."

Our anorexic FatLanders presented a different set of challenges.

Now that they were in FatLand, at least they weren't surrounded with unceasing pressure to be thin. And when they began eating more, they didn't have to worry about how much they gained. For the record, some of our anorexics were fat. But we soon saw that all of them needed something else besides positive reinforcement. They needed some cause or passion or talent to take up enormous amounts of energy that recovery released. Accordingly their counselors steered them to seek outlets for their energy.

Yet another component we added to their lives was that of family. Most of those with eating disorders, fat or not, had come along or had been sent or smuggled out by their families because the families knew that they would have little or no hope of recovery under the strict rationing and tax system ordained by the Health and Diet Laws. We arranged mentoring and group interaction systems for them.

We also instituted something a little more controversial: the block leader system. More than a few protested that such a measure smacked of the totalitarianism we were trying so hard to avoid. We assured the doubters that it was temporary.

The block leaders took it upon themselves to make sure that no one fell through the cracks if they needed any kind of help—physical, emotional, financial. The FatLand financial safety net was tight, even compared with the European social democracies: unemployment compensation, retraining, complete medical coverage, paid medical and parental leave for both parents. But it could not guarantee against depression. People do not always admit to being depressed or suicidal.

In the beginning we actually sent printed checklists around for people to assess their own wellbeing. Surprisingly we received more than half of them back—a return rate any survey would envy. Since they were overwhelmingly positive, we concluded that people who were upset or unhappy weren't filling them out.

One of the jobs of our block leaders was simply to mingle with people on the block. The main complaint they received was that Fat-Landers were scared to go out and talk to people. More than half the time this led to their encouraging FatLanders to go out, to get out of their apartments. They understood all too well that FatLanders had received so much harassment on the Other Side when they did walk in public that they were not able to let go of their old fears, even now that they were in FatLand. This part of their job proved both pleasant and rewarding as they saw FatLanders following their recommendations and actually becoming eager to walk the streets and sample the pleasures of window shopping and then buying, as they should have been able to do on the Other Side.

Yet another related part of the block leaders' task was either to help FatLanders let go of their pasts or to refer them for therapy when they judged that further help than they could give was necessary. FatLanders carried a lot of baggage from their previous lives on the Other Side: fear, resentment, guilt, sadness, eating disorders, depression. The results, however, of the block leaders' intercessions were little short of miraculous.

When FatLanders were able to talk about their problems and grief, and then to start walking or riding around FatLand—and often, reading about their difficulties—they shook off almost all of their reluctance, sadness and anxiety. This proved a boon for businesses, since FatLanders who walked or motored around town and started to have a taste for mingling were now consuming and appreciating all the good things establishments in FatLand had to offer. In turn the businesses hired more FatLanders, who in turn consumed more FatLand goods and services. It was a happy and rewarding cycle for individual FatLanders, for FatLand concerns, and for FatLand itself.

We could talk further about economic growth, medical supervision and therapy, but the block leaders ended up providing the very necessary glue of confidence to FatLanders. They typed tons and tons of reports. They offered their warmth and company twenty-four hours a day. They wore their Block Leader hats with pride. It is because of them that previously frightened and shy FatLanders gained the courage go to out, to socialize, shop, sing, eat, argue and dance, and thus encouraged others in turn to do so—even expected them to do so. Another wonderful cycle.

For the very first time in so many of their lives, FatLanders were able to say "Hello" to others and really mean it.

And what a thrill to see most of the anorexics and bulimics become happier eaters. In FatLand there was no pressure to be thin and no privilege points given for it. No one patted anyone on the back for losing weight—the very opposite view of that usually evinced on the Other Side. For at least half of the cases of anorexia and bulimia, just being in FatLand was enough to effect a permanent change in behaviors.

Because we had a ninety-nine percent success rate, the parents of anorectic children were granted grudging permission by the Health and Diet Boards to send their children to FatLand. The kicker, however, was that the children were expected to be sent back. However, in most cases we were able to keep the children. The Health and Diet Boards were simply not interested enough to request their return. The children who did go back did so at the behest of their parents. In three quarters of these cases, the parents ended up sending their children back again. The Health and Diet Boards actually acquiesced for one reason only: the presence of anorexics and bulimics was a severe embarrassment for them and a blow to their hopes of portraying themselves as "a nation in perfect health."

In those days all we had to do to embarrass Stark was to cite statistics on the incidence of anorexia and bulimia on the Other Side and how those who emigrated from the Other Side to FatLand were cured of both.

**Stark did request** meetings with us from time to time, mostly to see Margaret. This of course meant that those of us who took part had to obtain temporary visas from the USA. The process in itself was long and difficult.

At that point the USA didn't maintain diplomatic relations with FatLand. We had to go to the Swiss Legation office in Alberta. Two countries' airlines made stops in FatLand then: Italy and Samoa. However, Hawaiian Airlines, brand new and intrepid, also stopped in FatLand. Hawaii by and large didn't honor or implement most of the Health and Diet Laws. Soon FatLanders who weren't fans of the Colorado winters arranged to vacation in Hawaii for a couple of months. Hawaii even put into place a special category for FatLanders, who would travel to Hawaii but would not have their visas stamped. This way Hawaii did not incur punishment and FatLanders were not acting against international or FatLand laws.

When you arrived at the Swiss Legation office in Alberta, the staff people gazed at you as if you were from another planet when you sat down in the outside waiting area. "Mostly," a FatLand friend said, "because they're not used to seeing calm and happy people from the USA. They don't necessarily think you're from FatLand."

Nor did they. You waited until your name was called. They weighed you, but didn't say anything. It seemed to disappoint them when your "numbers"—blood pressure, cholesterol, triglycerides—were well within normal range, and this was the case most of the time with people from FatLand. It was fun to decimate their assumptions.

We never heard any reports of abuse or non-cooperation by Canadian doctors. Not one.

Then we braved the visa lines in Town Hall. Before the phasing-in of the Health and Diet Laws, they'd started to give visas online. But after the Canadian version was passed, the rules stipulated that each applicant had to be scanned and questioned in person.

**ALL THIS** to go from FatLand to Colorado, which was next door. And to The Laurels, minutes from the border.

It is difficult to describe the strangeness all of us experienced upon being weighed in the offices of government doctors in Canada. During our stay in FatLand most of us had forgotten what it was like to be appraised as a number on a scale—to be tyrannized by it, to accord it meaning and privilege over the way we felt in our own bodies. We had learned, some of us laboriously at first, to let go of any connections with numbers that terrified us. Our bodies flew free of them, then forgot them.

With all this, and remembering how it had been to be measured as a number on a scale, we knew we were infinitely better off than our fat brothers and sisters on the Other Side, in the USA. They were now ruled by people whose object it was to convert them to slimness, even though it had been shown over and over in different studies that it was impossible for ninety-five percent of "overweight" or "obese" people to lose weight permanently. So they were put on "programs"— in their own homes at first, and then, if they didn't lose weight or find ways to evade the weigh-ins, sent to the Re-Education Centers.

"Please come here, make your homes with us," we begged our friends and families, especially the ones who were fat. But either they didn't believe us or couldn't imagine what would occur under the Laws.

STARK TOOK untold pleasure in warning us each time about our own infrastructure, how in need of constant repair and maintenance it was, and how he could easily pull the plug on his not inconsiderable financial contribution to us. Helping us with one hand, undermining us with his CompleteFitness enterprise—not to mention sponsoring the Health and Diet Laws on the Other Side.

Margaret, of course, seemed to want little or nothing to do with him on the surface. But when people, including myself, saw them together, it was painfully obvious that there was an attachment.

FatAir had just begun to offer flights to and from Canada twice a day. The feelings with which those of us who were able to obtain seats on these flights boarded them were close to indescribable. One of our friends said that it was like being airlifted out of a flood. Indeed, one of the ads for FatAir put it like that.

> You've been stared at, frowned at, made to feel as if you're the wrong number on the scale. You've managed to find transport and get yourself to the FatAir Security Area. Then you're escorted to the gate for FatAir.
>
> Our ticket agents, FatLanders all, smile at you and shake your hand as they give you your choice of beverage after you've shown them your ticket. It's the first time all day that you feel like a person again.
>
> You sit down in the Waiting Area, which is adorned with pictures of sights and stores and attractions in FatLand. Soon you see other FatLanders arriving. You smile almost hesitantly. They smile back. You start talking. The time before your flight passes.
>
> When the boarding announcement comes, you line up in front of the access point for the plane. As you pass through the half door, a FatLand agent checks your ticket and smiles. You walk down the connecting ramp. As you reach the open door of the plane two air staffpeople, the captain, and the co-captain all smile and shake your hand. "Welcome to FatLand!" they say loudly and cheerfully.
>
> You feel your knees quaking in sheer relief and gladness as you try not to cry. "Thank you," you say as you walk into the spa-

cious FatAir Airbus 782.

Stretching out comfortably in your FatAir coach seat, you chat to the person next to you or listen to music or eat a snack of your choice during the hour flight.

When the seatbelt sign flashes on and the captain announces that the plane is descending and preparing to land, you close your eyes and lean back as the plane circles in.

Once you've collected your belongings, you exit from the plane and through the ramp.

The first person you see as you enter FatLand Territorial Airport is the Fatland Welcome Agent. She reaches out, shakes your hand, and smiles as she greets you with the words, 'Welcome home.'

FatAir. Because with us, you're home wherever you go.

IN A FEW YEARS FatAir had flights to most of the major cities in the USA. Its brave and courageous personnel took part in and were responsible for saving more than a few FatAndProud members—and their network of friends and family—who were in imminent danger of being incarcerated—"retained"—in Re-Education Centers and starved. Some of the Health and Diet Admins were perfectly aware that ninety to ninety-five percent of the people who lose weight on diets don't keep it off and often gain more back, but they insisted on keeping to this failed prescription and paradigm. People under the supervision of the Health and Diet Admins also got sick because they couldn't sleep or weren't receiving the nutrition they needed, even with vitamin pills, which didn't make up for what appetite suppression pills did to their systems.

FatAndProud, at great personal risk to themselves, kept track of as many members of their network as they could and managed to keep them out of sight of the Health and Diet Admins as long as they could. When it happened that one of them fell under the notice of the Health and Diet Administration they were sent, ideally, to Canada or Hawaii or other places via FatAir, if it was not possible to fly them or otherwise smuggle them into FatLand.

This is how it was done.

When a member or friend of FatAndProud's network was about to be sent to a Re-Education Center, FatAir received the numbers "42-2" on their screens. This meant that FatAndProud was preparing to smuggle the endangered individual to an airport at which FatAir had a contact waiting. Once the individual was smuggled safely to one of these airports, she or he—but most often she—was sequestered in the FatAir office complex, during which time she rested and was fed, then received a FatLand passport. A few factors now operated in her favor. Since FatAir had contacts and contracts in USA cities, but FatLand had no formal relations with the USA, there were no exchange or extradition policies that operated between them. Thus any FatAir facility in the USA became in effect a miniature FatLand—sovereign, discrete, unsearchable.

Because of the prejudices that had built up in the USA against fat people, the American staff and Admin personnel tended to lump them together without distinguishing any differences among them. If a fat person from the USA disappeared from her home city and turned up three or four or five days later under a different name, with dyed hair and contacts and wearing a FatAir uniform, Health and Diet Security had no clue as to how to locate her, and little inclination to try. Because of their own indoctrination, propaganda and prejudice, they were blind to the possibilities of fat people from the USA becoming FatAir staff or attendants. And they were not allowed to question FatAir people because FatLand and the USA had no diplomatic agreement.

I assisted in a couple of these rescues by escorting endangered fat people from the USA in taxis to airports served by FatAir. When I was able to move the individual into the security line for FatAir, with the signals prearranged, they would then remove her and escort her to the FatAir office complex after she reached close to the end of the line. When I would hear the FatAir staff say to her, "Welcome to FatLand," I felt the most tremendous waves of satisfaction  and knee-weakening relief I would ever know.

Another perk and good reason to fly FatAir was that FatAir never weighed its passengers. Of course FatAir took care to mention this prominently in its ads targeted to FatLand audiences, who comprised ninety percent of its market. But enough USA citizens started to appreciate non-weighed flying that they applied to FatAir for bookings. This both boosted FatAir  revenues and made it seem desirable and exclusive because it simply couldn't accept all the applications.

THE RESCUED fat people from the USA were given the choice of becoming citizens of FatLand—to which they would be flown as flight space allowed—or joining FatAir as staff. A counselor worked with them for as long as it took for them to decide. Most chose to live in FatLand, but a few opted to become FatAir agents and staff. In essence, both choices carried the same degree of safety.

Except in a couple of cases.

The first and most famous—or infamous—concerned a congressman from Virginia who insisted that God couldn't love fat people—that in order for fat people to "feel God's love," they had to become slim. He went so far as to target two prominent members of FatAndProud.

In most cases, being a prominent member of a nationally known organization buys you some protection from the vagaries of zealots. Not in this case, though. There was simply too much of an outcry against fat people for Congressman Mack's efforts to be seen as the determination of a zealot. Unfortunately for the two FatAndProud members, even at this early point, when there still existed border crossings and rights—-compromised, but still operational—for USA fat citizens who wished to emigrate to FatLand, they couldn't take advantage of any of them. What seemed so strange to so many of us was that the congressman kept blocking their efforts to cross into FatLand. We kept saying to each other, "You'd think that if he hated fat people so much and said that God hates them, he'd let them go to FatLand."

No sooner did the congressman excoriate the two members of FatAndProud for being unpatriotically fat than he started in on the entire FatLand territory itself, calling it a den of iniquity and a godless hell. However, this pronouncement did offend those of many faiths in the USA, and the Committee to Let Our People Go was born.

FatAir had just started, and as yet it was only flying to Montreal and Toronto. So the challenge became more complex because the two members, Alva and Maxine, had to cross into Canada first. For the sake of (relative) inconspicuousness, Alva was spirited in the backs of vans to Toronto, while Maxine was transported in chicken trucks to Vermont and then over the USA border to Montreal.

The two of them did reach their Canadian destinations more or less without incident. As soon as they reached the airports for their flights they were escorted through FatAir security lines and directly onto Fa-tAir flights. FatLand news outlets wanted to snap their arrival in Fat-Land, but had to be content with their descriptions of the trembling relief they both felt when they were enclosed in the FatAir Security Line and then again when they boarded their respective FatAir flights.

Their arrival in FatLand touched off huge celebrations and parties and even a few concerts. And that, you'd think, was the end of the matter.

But Congressman Mack was not one to let his quarry rest and relax in their new home. No sirree, not he. Upon being told that an invasion of FatLand was out of the question, he sent drone flights over the area of FatLand in which the two women from the USA were staying. He kept writing op-ed columns and posts on why the two FatAndProud leaders who had escaped owed it to God and Country to turn them-selves in.

This was when the FatLand Safe House project was begun. Since the drones were unarmed and even Stark wasn't about to have FatLand invaded—at least not yet—there really wasn't a whole lot the honor-able congressman could do to the two escapees from the USA except harass them.

Of course this harassment was completely unacceptable to FatLand-ers. So besides the Safe House project, and a new mini-business selling dartboards with the congressman's head on them, FatLand launched a semi-but-not-quite-underground project to hack and harass the Face-book and Twitter pages of the congressman. One of the ways they did this was to post pictures of the congressman with curvaceous and lus-cious cuties of FatLand, changing them every few hours.

The congressman finally stopped his campaign against the two Fa-tAndProud members and escapees two days later.

A side effect of the affair was that some men in the USA launched a not-very-underground site for men who desired fat women, but hosted it offshore, since such sites were forbidden under the Health and Diet Laws.

The women who posed next to Congressman Mack accrued a 500- to 1000-percent increase in their Facebook and Twitter traffic and had themselves "pinned" on Pinterest.

When the first Safe House was completed the two new FatLand citizens chose to stay in it for a while. Eventually they moved to another part of FatLand.

By then there were no more drones.

# 2045

**FROM THE FATLAND ARCHIVAL AND HISTORICAL BOARD:**

It is highly recommended that the interviewer use FatLand transport because no vehicles may be parked within half a mile of the Safe House Zone.

Only one interviewer may conduct the interview.

**"I HAVE DETERMINED,"** Dash said that evening, "that I am probably the least qualified person to conduct this interview. Unfortunately I am also the best from a security standpoint."

"How do you figure that?" Roberta asked.

They sat in a large, noisy buffet-type restaurant not far from Roberta's apartment in the southern area of FatLand.

"No one will try to follow me after I conclude the interview. I'm not a FatLand citizen."

"Are you sure of that?" Roberta asked.

"What can they do? Yell at the Indian government?" He raised a forkful of mashed potatoes to his mouth.

"I guess the 'they' here is Stark?" Janine asked.

They all glanced at each other.

"We can't be sure," Roberta said. "That strange call in the hotel may have been a wrong number."

"They had to go through the system," Dash pointed out.

Janine said, "I think we should accompany you up to the Safe Zone and wait nearby."

"Absolutely not," Dash said. "Anyone want more rolls?"

# Angela

**As FatLanders, and members of a territory,** we were not technically allowed to call ourselves citizens. We did anyway.

There was a long discussion and passage of a counter-law early in the history of FatLand, around one month or so after the territory was formally won and declared. It read: "For purposes of national allegiance and welfare, every FatLander who was born in FatLand, or sought and was granted asylum in FatLand, or who successfully applied for and underwent FatLand's residential acclimatization process, shall be called and considered a citizen."

**Stark,** of course, was livid at the time, taking out op-eds in every large news organ and blog around. For once, it did no good. Perhaps this was one of the factors behind FatLand's Mondo-Size Rebellion. I grant that it might have occurred anyway, but not with such form and strength. The embarrassing thing is that Stark was right in his view of the improvements needed to serve the mondo-size people, but the board wouldn't agree for a long while because of the expense.

Sometimes, at my most paranoid, I believe that someone on the board was purposely pushed by Stark to seem to disagree with him so FatLand would seem to look bad by denying necessary services to its mondo-size citizens and thus look as if it were discriminating against them. At other times, however, I doubted that even Stark would go that far. After all, FatLand was experiencing a temporary shortfall in funds due to the FatLand Cyber Security Project, which guaranteed that FatLand could not be hacked, and the FatLand Air Defense Project, directed against drones and missiles. These projects were deemed so necessary that taxes had to be raised. The problem was that a couple of people on the board at the time refused to raise taxes on the top bracket, a measure which would have made up all of the shortfall—and would also have stipulated heavier taxes on enterprises partly or completely owned by Stark. And this is why I believed—at times—that Stark orchestrated the rebellion of the mondo-size.

He claimed, unfortunately quite correctly, that mondo-size Fat-Landers needed their services updated, and in some cases redone completely. On the other hand, he refused to pay the extra taxes that would have guaranteed the availability of funds for this project.

So the new taxes fell disproportionately on the second and third brackets of taxpaying FatLanders, who were furious. And the mondo-size people were extremely angry because their needs weren't being met. Hence the Mondo-Size Rebellion.

The term "mondo-size" was originally used by FatAndProud on the Other Side to distinguish people who fell in a certain weight category. Usually the cutoff was somewhere between three hundred fifty and four hundred pounds. There was at times a connotation of disability attached to the term, which led to its being used mostly in circles of fat people. It was revived ironically when FatLand was created, in order to designate people who needed facilities, vehicles and services geared toward the largest bodies.

The Mondos looked to Paul as their leader, even though he was no longer present—even though most of them hadn't known him at all—because he was definitely one of the largest people who had inhabited FatLand, and probably the most brilliant. He was the one who once said to Angela, "Could you love a mondo man?" Not quite knowing what he meant, she said, "Does that mean some kind of world traveler?" It was overheard, got passed around, and became kind of a snarky legend, after which some of the larger folk in FatLand began to call themselves Mondos. The name clicked and spread.

One pleasant summer morning—and summer mornings were often very pleasant in FatLand because of its location and lack of pollution—Fabrey Boulevard, off Howell Terrace, was inundated by mondo-size people, about half on wheelchairs and scooters. From quite a distance away you could hear, "FatLand steals and FatLand lies. Doesn't want the Mondo-Size."

"Say what?" I said on first hearing, then clicked Margaret's speed dial on my smartphone.

"It's been in the works for a while," she said.

"How long?"

"Most of a year."

"Why now?"

"Stark encouraged some of our Mondo-Sizers to express their needs."

I sighed. We needed to be a lot more vigilant about maintaining the bikeways and wheelways. We needed to build more mondo-size bathrooms and make sure that all restaurants and doctors' offices had the latest mondo-size equipment and seating and technology. He just pushed it.

"He wants to talk to you."

I looked around. One of the main avenues and a bridge were completely blocked. If this wasn't dealt with quickly, it could become a major embarrassment for FatLand. "Why me? I'm not even on the board."

"He says he knew you'd say that."

"Well, he's right. But I'm still not on the board."

"He says you have them by the balls."

"Charming image. I suppose I'd better talk to him."

"Agreed. You want to come up?"

"Sure. Warn me somehow if I stray into forbidden territory."

"Angela."

"Winston."

"Thank you for getting in touch with me."

"What did you wish to discuss?"

"I have an offer for you."

"And that is?"

"I will build the facilities your mondo-size infrastructure so badly needs if you will go away."

"First of all, very kind of you. But go away where?"

"Wherever you wish."

"And why am I going?"

"So a mondo-size person can finally be on the board."

"But I'm not even on the board currently."

"Doesn't matter. The mondo-size person will be loyal to me."

"Ah. So this way the mondo-size infrastructure gets renovated, the board gets a mondo-size member, you get a loyal supporter on the board, and I go away and trouble you no more."

"In a nutshell. And your airfare and apartment will be funded."

"By?"

"Me."

"I must say that for a conniving plutocrat, you are quite generous."

"That's me. So where would you like to go?"

"What if I don't choose to go?"

"Then you would instead live as my guest in my stunningly beautiful Colorado complex."

"So you really aim to get me out of FatLand, no matter what."

"Just remember that someone dear to you spent the last few years of his life as happily as possible."

"Yes. I suppose I should thank you for that."

"Of course. You have a minute to decide."

"I'll go," I said. "But I have to sell my place. And I have to say goodbye to people."

"A week."

"Yippee."

"And Margaret will bill you as a foreign correspondent for the *Fat-Land Free Press*. It will fit perfectly."

"You have it all worked out," I said.

"I always do."


I HOPED that Stark wouldn't have someone start a rumor that I didn't like mondo-sized people because I'd been attached to one who had left, or something ridiculous like that but difficult to disprove.

Ironically, FatLand produced very few mondo-sized people on its own. Lack of stigma, lack of emphasis on weight, lack of weight cycling from dieting, movement options for all, opportunities to choose food, lack of stress, excellent medical coverage and care, financial security— for whatever reason or mix of reasons, the distribution of weights of adults in FatLand became similar to those in the USA after the first five years or so, but with two important differences: there were very few skinny people—the bottom of the bell curve—and very few mondo-sized people—the top of the curve. As birth rates grew and mortality rates continued to fall, FatLand experienced a modest boom in population. It might have been even higher, but FatLanders didn't believe in very large families. Two or three children were the norm.

FatLanders tended to be spiritually inclined, but not religious. They did like to gather for celebratory festivals and found excuses for them several times a month. The time of the season was a cause for celebration, as were people's birthdays, anniversaries, first years of puberty, menopause, marriages, divorces, partnerships. All they had to do was to get a permit to use public space and make sure that some kind of security—not necessarily police—was provided. As a matter of fact, since police often didn't have a whole lot to do in FatLand because the crime rate was remarkably low, people tended to function as security personnel between jobs. Security Consciousness Training was a good business in itself in FatLand, and yielded a Security Certificate in six months, with the training paid for.

People who became unemployed in FatLand were automatically guaranteed a stipend for as long as they were unemployed. It provided them with enough to purchase food, pay rent and utilities, and have a couple of parties per month. The payment of stipends was also made easier because FatLanders used their excellent transportation system regularly and didn't have to depend on their vehicles for daily transport. Many observed that they preferred to ride the FatLand Transport System because it was so much easier to get on and ride than to squeeze their way in and out of cars—FatLand did not have auto manufacturing facilities. Many FatLanders did, however, own vans and pickups. Very few used sport utility vehicles because they did not vacation nearby but further away, where FatAir took them.

Every person who became unemployed received career counseling at least until she obtained some kind of employment. Workers' associations also furnished services, especially if the unemployed person wished to become employed in the fields they represented. Some Fat-Landers appreciated the employment counseling so much that they maintained a relationship with their counselors and continued to request sessions and tips even when they were again employed.

Another good way to secure employment between or after jobs was to become a member of the Fatland Nature Corps. Members learned to garden, landscape, to care for parklands, to identify and nurture flora and fauna, to report on activities of animals in certain areas, to take soil samples, to care for rivers and riverland and lakes, and, if they wished, to report on and chart weather patterns. Some FatLanders liked being in the Nature Corps so much that they made it their occupation and career. Besides everything else, Nature Corps members said, it gave them a good reason to be outside most of the day and to get lots of walking in.

Not that FatLanders usually needed much of an excuse to be outside. This was yet another freedom FatLand afforded—being outside, walking around, exercising in whatever fashion one wished without being belittled or shamed. Because so many FatLanders took eager advantage of this freedom, there were always FatLanders walking from place to place or just walking, day or night. This was yet another reason that the crime level in FatLand was so very low. It was extremely difficult to do anything in FatLand without someone seeing you. And FatLanders were not a quiet or passive bunch. Anyone seen doing something that seemed questionable would be quickly and politely asked if he or she needed assistance. About 99 percent of the time these questionable behaviors carried plausible and understandable explanations.

Guns of any kind were forbidden in FatLand except to a very few police, certain security personnel, and customs staff. And even they were forbidden from carrying them when they were off duty.

FatLand and FatLanders kept up with tech and automated devices and innovated and invented quite a few. Not only the famous Smart-Wheels—wheelchairs that turned into scooters, then flying scooters—but also DishBright, which not only washed and dried dishes, but stacked them, and ClothesBright, which did the same for clothes. Fat-Land programmers, following in my dear one's footsteps, invented interactive programming languages that spoke with each other and were translatable into human speech. FatLand engineers created bridges that shut down automatically if more than a certain amount of wheeled traffic started to cross. Around 2020, flying lanes started to become part of the vehicular traffic—lanes also invented by FatLand traffic coordinators with the help of the inventors of the smart vehicles which were programmed to phase in and out of flying.

As a matter of fact, FatLanders, released from bodily stigma, seemed in a hurry to make up for all the years that they had been belittled and discriminated against, with the result that the FatLand economy burgeoned. Associations of like-minded people, staff, workpeople—usually but not only centered on workplaces—made sure that companies maintained representation and fair and pleasant conditions for their staff and workers. One main feature was furniture that held and seated people up to 700 pounds comfortably, although as stated previously, most FatLanders did not weigh anything near this.

Often workers actually owned parts of the businesses at which they worked. This made for a strong physical and emotional investment in their workplaces. FatLanders tended to like anything that would guarantee their legitimacy and their right simply to live and die in one place. There were too many memories of places that had not allowed them to do so.

# 2045

"**Do you think we should follow him?**" Janine texted Roberta.

"He's a big boy. At least in age."

"Yes, but I have a bad feeling about this."

Roberta texted, "Did you ever play FatLand SpyClimb when you were younger?"

"Video or actual?"

"Both."

"Mostly video."

"We did both. My parents wanted us to get exercise. Now that I think about it, I wonder if they were also part of FIN."

"Can you ask them?"

"They're traveling right now. But that shouldn't matter."

"When did they come to FatLand?"

"2014. The year of the Great Migration. The year that the Health and Diet Laws took effect. When the USA built most of the Re-Education Centers. When did yours come?

"They didn't."

"Then how did you get here?"

"My biological parents sent me over with friends. They were scared for me. I was a chubby little kid. They didn't know what would happen."

"Why didn't they come?"

"They had a jewelry store. They didn't see any reason to move. They were both thin."

"Are they still around?"

"No."

"I'm sorry."

"They were sent to a Re-Education Center when they tried to get my brother out."

"What happened to your brother?"

"He was sent to Hawaii. They didn't enforce most of the Health and Diet Laws there, as you know."

"I remember seeing the Map of Enforcement in high school, when we learned about the treatment of fat people in the USA after the passage of the Health and Diet Laws. Do you still communicate with him?"

"Actually I didn't, but I'm thinking that since the Anti-Diet Revolution maybe we should. I didn't want to get him in trouble. I mean, I know Hawaii didn't enforce the Laws, but you never could be sure of who might be around or monitoring."

"So you were raised by your parents' friends?" Roberta asked. They were now talking aloud.

"Yes."

"Did you know they weren't your parents?"

"I sort of did, but they didn't say a lot about it. Then one day they took me aside and said they loved me more than anything. And they told me I was their precious Janine. They said they had bad news about my birth parents."

"Did they know why they died?"

"It was kind of ironic. They went on a hunger strike to get better treatment for those who were detained in the Centers. Can you imagine? All the Re-Ed Center people thought it was a big joke. Except for one of them. He was the one who sent my parents' friends the news. I always wanted to talk to him more, too."

"Do you know where he is?"

"Strangely enough, someone I talked to said he might be in Fat-Land."

ROBERTA SMARTTEXTED her mother: "Mom, this came up in connection with a project. Were you or dad ever in FIN—FatLand Intelligence Network?"

Her mother smarttexted back within a minute. "Why?"

Roberta responded, "We were discussing the early days of FatLand, and I remembered how we used to play FatLand SpyClimb and that you wanted me to play it outside, not just by video."

A couple of minutes passed. Then a message came. "Truth by Fat-Land and for FatLand. Does that answer you?"

"Both of you?" Roberta typed.

"Yes."

She wanted very much to ask more, but was not allowed to do so. She contented herself with, "Having a good time?"

"Very," her mother answered.


THE NEXT MORNING Dash said to them, "You weren't planning anything strange, were you?"

"We're not going to follow you," Roberta said.

# Angela

IT PROBABLY WOULDN'T BE TOO FARFETCHED to say that for most FatLanders, FatLand had become paradise. To walk into the street as a once-hated person, hated only for your shape, and encounter not hate but a general and peaceful appreciation of your place as a citizen of your territory, and a "Hello" and "Good morning" as you sauntered or strolled or dawdled—

The FatLand doctors were astonished to see FatLanders almost right before their very eyes shed heart problems for no discernible reason. Lengthy studies concluded that this occurrence was either caused or aided substantially by the lack of hatred and stigma in their environment. And since most of the FatLand doctors themselves experienced quick and staggering improvements in their own heart functions and strength, also for no clearly definable reason, they couldn't doubt the evidence literally right before their eyes.

There were, however, a few groups who didn't immediately experience the peace and ease and empowerment of living in FatLand: the mondo-sized, the slim people, and a third group who for a long time went unidentified and unnamed because their condition was neither recognized nor named.

After the uprising of the mondo-sized, their needs were taken much more into account in the FatLand budget as well. New mondo-size-friendly buildings, transport, stores, restaurants, even medical offices were built. There were also mondo-sized bathrooms and furniture-making concerns, as well as vehicular innovation think tanks, that were launched. Stark bought the buildings and outfitted them originally, but turned them over to mondo-sized buyers and interior designers. By dint of newly proud mondo-sized attendants and counselors, the mondo-sized learned to take pride in both their acceptance and accomplishments.

With all this support Stark furnished to the support and improvement of the position of the mondo-sized in FatLand, you'd think that he would have updated and changed the message of the ads for his Complete Fitness chain, and would now be welcoming the mondo-sized. There were indeed a few mondo-size gyms run by someone named Sandor Forman. But Stark pushed a weight loss emphasis for his chain at the very same time that he was empowering the mondo-sized in FatLand.

And this as much as anything else sealed Stark's lack of acclaim in FatLand and from FatLanders. It was his *ignis fatuus*, his failing, his key flaw. Some saw it as lame stupidity, some as a blind spot, some as a fabulous lack of self-knowledge—especially those who believed rumors that he had a mondo-sized lover. I even said as much to him in my one attempt to get him to understand himself, shortly before I left.

"You love a woman who is beautiful and fat," I said. "You've invested millions in our infrastructure. You've done more for the mondo-sized of FatLand than almost any other person around. And yet you keep threatening FatLanders and people on the Other Side with ridiculous and wrongheaded and scientifically disproven schemes to get us to lose weight. You must know by now that weight loss comes back as increased fat ratio to muscle. It's so much healthier for us to walk and garden and throw snowballs than it is to exhaust ourselves dieting and exercising in the vain hope of changing our body types. Why don't you convert your diet message to one of health? You certainly have the resources to do so."

But of course Stark operated in a very different world and by a very different set of rules. According to his power-driven, control-seeking logic, anything that made him look vulnerable or uncertain couldn't be countenanced. "Have no time to argue this," he replied. "Have a great trip."

I code-texted Dave—who was now married to Esther—my new address. I told him that I was on assignment for the *FatLand Free News* and would be gone for a long time. I wished them both well and sent them a set of bowls made by FatLand potters.

Slimmer people were at first a conundrum. Of course genetically it made sense that at least a small percentage of FatLanders would be slim or slimmer. I am sorry to say that at times there was an undertow of resentment and discrimination, as well. Slimmer children were sometimes harassed at school; slimmer adults were harassed in their workplaces. Parents pushed their slim children to eat and gain weight, then stopped when their efforts proved vain, as they were about ninety-nine percent of the time.

The board determined that a lot of enlightenment and consciousness-raising would have to take place. They launched, among other things, a contest for the best banner showing FatLanders of all sizes, including both children and adults. The winning banner featured twelve children and twelve adults of all sizes dancing in a circle (considered non-hierarchical, as well). Classes on FatLand Citizenship and Equality were instituted in all schools, including FatLand University. Equality counselors were assigned to both the name callers and the name-called. FatLand newspapers featured editorials on the subject of the importance of equality and tolerance for FatLanders of all sizes.

Within a year, the situation stabilized. Within two years, the incidence of harassment of slimmer people was down seventy-five percent. Harassment didn't stop altogether in subsequent years, but the number of reported incidents remained fairly low two per year among FatLand's 400,000 population.

# 2045

DASH PARKED IN THE SAFE HOUSE DESIGNATED parking area. He showed his passport and the two letters from the FatLand Archival and Historical Board. The guard stamped the letters and put in a call to the house he would be visiting.

During the previous year, FatAndProud and two members of the FatLand Board had teamed up to kidnap Sandor Foreman, Stark's former partner, to save him from jail time in the USA, where Stark had leveled charges against him of improperly terminating a business agreement. Since then Stark had sent drones to harass the FatAndProud members who were housed in the Safe Houses after that risky operation. Guards in the Safe House area and around the Safe Houses themselves had been doubled, and a high wall already in place on one side of the Safe House area near the parking lot was refortified.

Dash presented his documents again. A gate lifted and he passed through. Consulting the address and directions on the map on his phonetab, he made his way to Safe House 26.

He showed his documents to the invisible eye and reader. The front door swung open. "Please proceed left to the common area," an intercom ordered in tastefully quiet tones.

As he stood in front of the common area door, another female voice intoned, "Please press A-7." He did so. The door slid open from both sides.

The room was dimmer than he had expected, and he blinked twice before he was able to see Shermaine, former president of FatAndProud, who had been forced to remain in FatLand after the rescue she and others had carried out the previous year.

"Hello," she said.

"Hello." Dash now saw that she was seated on a rather fetching sofa at the other end of the spacious common room. He walked over to her and put out his hand.

Her handshake was strong and vigorous. "Nice to see you," she said.

"It is a honor to meet you," he said.

"Thanks."

"You're famous for the rescue," he said. "And for your role and position in FatAndProud."

She laughed. "When I got here, I wrote in my journal that it was weird, being thought of as a hero. The weirdest thing was not being insulted or attacked in the streets. Everyone was so eager to be kind. Then, when I was here for a little longer, I realized that people are actually kind to each other here. They don't need an incentive."

"Is FatAndProud still active on the Other Side, as they call it here?"

"Very. They've taken a major role in helping people transition and adjust now that the Health and Diet Laws have been repealed."

"What a change for them."

"Sometimes I can hardly believe it. It seems like yesterday when we were texting and telling each other which places to avoid so they wouldn't pick us up and send us to Centers."

"Were you and the other members of FatAndProud shocked when the Health and Diet Laws passed?"

"Well, the Laws themselves seemed to come from nowhere. But they didn't, really. They passed a slew of laws a couple of years before that. Made it difficult to obtain any kind of women's health or reproductive care. The books mostly mention abortions, but that was only part of it. You couldn't even get contraceptives without a hassle. Then they passed laws that police could strip-search you without cause, and then especially if you were outside after a certain hour. It's like they were closing in on you from all sides to keep you in your house and pregnant. And then, just around this time they started the anti-obesity campaigns."

"Tell me more about those," Dash said.

"Oh, Lord." Shermaine leaned back on the comfortable couch. Dash realized that her beautiful silk dress was similar in pattern to the cream and gold print on which she reclined. "Show after show screaming that "obesity"—they meant "fat people"—was the cause of everything from lower productivity to global warming. Even people who should have known better were praising shows that abused and tortured fat people in the name of weight and fitness, or so they called it. The contestants lost weight, then gained back every pound and often more. Then they started ordering the contestants who didn't lose weight to run fifty miles. Some of them died."

Dash and Shermaine sat quietly for a minute. Then he said, "When did you all realize that the Health and Diet Laws were going to be dangerous?"

"When the Re-Ed Centers and monitoring started. A few of us realized quickly. Some went to FatLand. The rest of us? We still couldn't believe that the Supreme Court wasn't challenging and nullifying them. The problem was that no one would bring a case. Then we tried, but by then the Supreme Court wouldn't hear it.

"The first part of the Health and Diet Acts came in 2012, after it was railroaded through Congress. At the time it was like it embarrassed them to admit that the USA's medical system cost more than any other system, but fell way short of being the best to help people remain healthy. So they blamed fat people for driving up costs and announced that the Health and Diet Laws would be put in place over a period of two years to make people "fit." They really meant "slimmer," since they knew by then that fat people could be fit."

"So originally the Health and Diet Laws were the brainchild of the insurance industry to scapegoat people so the industry could maintain the status quo and not undergo reforms?"

"Not only the insurance industry. The diet, fitness and pharmaceutical industries were behind them, too. This was right at the time when the belief in health at every size was starting to spread. Scientists were discovering or confirming that people have setpoint weights—or a range of weights—that go with them through life. They can vary by a certain amount, but people's bodies tend to return to the setpoints.

"So what did the Fitness Consortium, their new ad hoc group, do? It trotted out every outworn theory, every disproven hypothesis, every anti-fat cliché we could imagine. Not only global warming being caused by fat people. Let's see—we weren't mentally effective, our ba-

bies were unhealthy, we ate only fried meats, we weren't good lovers."
She laughed. "At least a third of those people had fat lovers on the side.
Added hypocrisy to the lies, besides everything else."

"What did FatLand do when the Re-Education and monitoring
programs were instituted?" Dash asked.

A tear coursed down Shermaine's cheek. "Funny," she said. "I
thought I'd be able to deal with that question. I guess I was trying to
avoid it, though. Even now."

"If you don't want to—"

"Oh, no, no. I want to. That's where some of our real heroes were.

"We had an inkling about the first part of the Health and Diet Acts
when it was passed. So we weren't completely shocked by the weigh-ins
and the fees and the all-but-forbidden foods. That was in 2012.

"What did shock us was the second part, which went into effect
in 2014. That's when it felt as if they'd gone completely nuts. It was
bad enough that Congress wanted to push probes up us every time
we needed any reproductive care. Now they wanted to send us to Re-
Education Centers to lose weight. They almost succeeded in passing an
Electronic Monitor Law which would have put electronic tech devices
on all of us, linking up to a central monitor so they would know exactly
what we'd eaten and when."

"For fat people or for others as well?"

"If your BMI was over 30. If it was between 25 and 30, you had to
report to a Diet Admin Counselor every week."

"But they didn't pass it."

"Failed by one vote—a Republican senator from Maine who said
she could not in good conscience report to her constituents that she
had allowed such a law to pass. She lost her seat at the end of that term,
and she'd served five in a row. But instead they built the Re-Ed Centers—ten times worse, to my mind."

"Were you in one?" Dash asked.

"No, thank the Lord. They gave me pills instead. Made me nuts,
had me climbing the walls."

"Did you lose weight?"

She laughed. "Hell, no. They hated that. Here I was, half-starved
and crazier than a loon, but I sure wasn't losing any weight. So they
upped the dose. Makes perfect sense, right? The first dose wasn't work-

ing, so they prescribed more of what wasn't working. It's like multiplying 150,000 by zero. You still get zero. Friends told me I had to get out of there. Between you and me, I was darned glad when they asked me to help with Mr. Foreman's rescue. Even if I died, I figured it couldn't be worse than what I was going through."

"Would it have been any better in a Re-Ed Center?"

"Depends on what you call 'better.' No, I would not have liked to fight for extra food the guards threw into our rooms and not wear any clothes while I was fighting as the guards took pictures."

"What?"

"You heard me."

"Did you have that corroborated?"

"Someone smuggled a personal journal and some pictures through. Then a FatAndProud person actually had herself assigned to that center."

"Do you have any idea of when that was?"

"Let me think. That was around 2041. Just about four years ago. Just before folks started to protest."

"What made them start to protest?"

"I remember what it was. The headline was banned in the USA, but it got out on the net anyway. About FatLanders living longer than Americans. Ha ha. I'll bet Stark was fit to be tied when he saw that one. That's when people started to figure that the hell they were going through and the hell the USA had become wasn't worth it. They wanted their country back. That's what the signs said."

"Did they do away with the Re-Ed Centers then?"

"People tore them down. Like with the Bastille. That was great. I saw one of them after people trashed it. All the patients were running around, opening all the freezer units. They threw all the medical equipment into a big fire. All the patients and people from outside were dancing around it."

"What about the guards?"

"They gave the guards the choice of joining them or running. Two guards joined them. They said they'd only taken positions as guards to avoid being assigned as patients. One of them was smuggling in food to some of the patients when he could."

"And the rest?"

"They ran. No one wanted to risk his/her life for a Re-Ed Center."

"Was this the first destruction of a Re-Ed Center?"

"Second, I think."

"Do you ever want to go back, now that the Health and Diet Laws have been repealed?

"I think about it every day. Most of my friends and relatives are still there. The FatAndProud people keep in touch with me. I hear constantly from folks asking if I'd like to go back now."

"Why do you stay?"

"Could you turn off your recorder?"

Dash turned it off.

"I don't know if you know this, but right after we staged the rescue of Sandor, and we were across the border and put into Safe Houses, we wanted to celebrate, so we had a picnic. In the woods, right near the Safe Houses, Stark sent drones over us. We had to come right back."

"But wouldn't it thus be more difficult for Stark to find you someplace in the USA?"

"FIN—FatLand Intelligence Network—talked to us. They keep in touch with people on The Other Side. They say that as long as Stark is around, he will try to silence us. And at least they can guard us here. Besides," she laughed, "I guess they don't want to lose their heroes. They even invented medals for us, would you believe it."

Dash looked at Shermaine. "Is the rescue operation public knowledge? Can you talk about it?"

"They told us not to."

"*Ahan.*" Dash veered into South Asian English for a second. Then he looked into Shermaine's striking almond eyes. "A man could get trapped in your eyes, you know that?"

She chuckled. "So I've been told. Now that I sleep again. Can I interest you in your choice of pastry and beverage?"

He circled the skin around her wrist with a finger. "I want you," he said. "Not a pastry." He took her hand and propelled her from the couch.

**An hour or so later,** Dash surveyed Shermaine's body in the warm, low lamplight. "I've never seen anything so beautiful," he said softly. "Your skin has the softest planes and the sweetest curves I could imagine. I want to be in you so much that I'm stopping myself for the sheer pleasure of anticipating."

Shermaine took Dash's finger and circled her right breast with it. "Don't stop now, dear."

Dash lowered his mouth to her nipple and started to lick and tease the skin around it. Shermaine cried out. His tongue played around her nipple, then dived into it. She moaned happily. His fingers started to inch up her thigh, circling, rubbing, squeezing, occasionally pinching. As his fingers made their way up his mouth worked its way down her stomach, licking. He sent his tongue into soft ripples and valleys now salty with sweat.

"God," she whispered.

His fingers and tongue finally met.

# Angela

I **SHOULD TALK ABOUT THE PEOPLE** in the very last category—
the one I have not yet named—but it is easier to talk about, say, the
FatLand tax code, which pleased most FatLanders because under it,
there were no taxes for people who earned under one million dollars.
The first millionaire bracket was taxed at three percent. Billionaires—
and FatLand boasted several—were taxed at twenty percent. It should
be emphasized that there were no loopholes or deductions. About half
of the collected revenue went toward schooling, from pre-kindergarten
to university.

I think also of the one national "duty" of FatLanders, which occurred—still occurs—as each FatLander turns thirteen. The FatLand
"coming of age" ceremony proclaims thirteen-year-olds citizens of Fatland. Each thirteen-year-old FatLander takes an oath to be loyal to
FatLand and to serve the best interests of FatLand "as long as you shall
dwell within."

Since FatLand has no army or armed forces, the "best interests" of
FatLand are usually interpreted in these stipulated tasks: a) graduating
with an education degree to teach in FatLand for a certain number of
years; b) carrying out a project or writing a paper about some aspect
of FatLand life with the object of having it published in a journal or
newspaper; c) training to be on a FatLand sports team or a professional
sports person or coach or counselor; d) performing/accomplishing a
FatLand arts project; e) becoming a member of the FatLand Patrol.

Thus far, FatLand has not separated into political parties, although there are certainly factions. Not standing factions, though—they seem to group and regroup around different issues.

I'VE BEEN PROCRASTINATING, hemming and hawing, trying to sneak up on this topic slowly, gently. I've even been listening to music in an effort to relax myself, to ease into it. Where I live now there are quite a number of young people who play music and dance and talk and drink until all hours. It helps.

This has to do with Jimmy.

If you remember, Jimmy was one of the original housemates in *Living Fat and Happy.* Later he became a double agent for FatLand who served as a border guard at one of the FatLand-USA crossings.

At first I assumed that he was interested in being a member and then a proud citizen of FatLand because he was a Fat Liberation activist.

What I didn't understand at the time was that Jimmy was searching for the answer to a certain question he had about his body and its responses. And no, I don't mean why he appreciated women by the roomful.

I found out more when we were having our FatLand Winter Carnival. Winter was warmer than it used to be, but still cold enough to feature ice sculptures and ice skating. All FatLand celebrations featured food, and I'd worked with a few FatLand restaurants to come up with a pleasing and eclectic menu for events such as this. Christmas goodies—turkey, plum pudding, pasties, Christmas cookies, egg nog—took up one section. Latkes, jelly donuts, chocolate Chanukah "gelt" were on the left side. Mithai and biryani—Diwali fare—occupied part of the right side. Kwanzaa foods—collard greens, black eyed peas, fried chicken, ribs, sweet potato pie—took up a section in the middle of the carnival. Ramadan evening goodies—dates, yogurt with honey, kebabs, roti bread—made their appearance nightly toward the front.

Most attendees partook of quite a few of the carnival offerings, with the result that they walked away either full or very full—occasionally, too full. I myself was having a rather good time going back and forth among sections and tables, greeting people, sampling goodies, also making sure that the items were replenished when they ran out.

Someone in a hooded coat stood near me. He put turkey on his plate with some artisanal bread from one of the bakeries. Then, as he reached out to add a cookie, his right hand stopped. He reached again. His hand stopped again. His eyes and mouth went slack. He edged away from the table and sat down at a side table. He put the plate with the bread and turkey in front of him, but didn't eat any of it.

By this time I realized who the hooded man was and sat down next to him. "Jimmy," I whispered. "It's okay. I won't say anything. I'm glad you could be here for a little while."

He didn't turn in my direction. "It's not okay."

"What? Why not?"

"I don't want to talk about it now. Will you be in your condo later?"

"Yes." I didn't question by now how he knew.


THE FESTIVITIES rolled on. I felt strange and lost my appetite, something I usually didn't do even when I was sick. I helped with cleanup and thanked the suppliers and food servers and handed out certificates of appreciation to all the participating restaurants and bakeries. By the time I made it back, it was after eleven.

Jimmy stood near the condo door. I opened it quickly and motioned him in. "Coffee or tea?" I said.

"Coffee."

He was sitting fully up on one of my couches. He took a sip of coffee. Then he asked, "Have you ever heard of the Ceres Piper Project?"

"No."

"The idea was to make supposedly obese children slim by implanting electrodes into their brains and hypnotizing them not to eat certain foods at the same time. Sort of a one-two punch."

"So did it work?"

"The children didn't eat the foods. But their body types didn't change. The part that upset them was that they hated certain foods, but they didn't know why."

"But you said they didn't remember."

"Then how did you find out?"

"My parents got me into the project."

"And then?"

"It wasn't exactly what they bargained for. Oh, I hated all the foods they wanted me to hate. I still don't like ice cream or cake or even potato chips. Some of the FatLand health nuts look to me as their model.

What they don't realize—"

"Tell me."

"When I was about ten or so, I started to throw tantrums. I also had trouble sleeping at night. My parents went with me to psych people, therapists, acupuncturists, homeopaths, you name it. None of them had a clue. I got so violent at times I almost strangled my brother. That's when my parents sent me to this military-type boarding school. My phys ed instructors were really impressed with me. They didn't even care that I was 'overweight.' I ended up majoring in phys ed in college. I found that when I played football or worked out, I forgot about those strange feelings. But other weird symptoms started to occur. Every time I looked at ice cream or candy, the forbidden foods, I felt as if I were in this deep void. As if something was coming to swallow me. It was worse than that, but this is the only way I can describe it."

"So how did you put it together?"

"The FatLand Board picked me to go underground as a double agent. At first I just thought of it as an honor. They told me to find out anything and everything about Stark. So I read. I figured out his habits, where he hung out, where he lived, what he liked, what he hated.

Then one night when I couldn't sleep, I started to read about different weight loss methods on the Other Side, as I was asked to do. The listing for the Ceres Piper Project was obscure. It was one line next to WLS. The Health and Diet Administration in the USA had commissioned a study on it."

"My God."

"Yeah. So I kept reading. That's when things started to click. The more I read, the more sense it all made."

"So what did you do then?"

"I went to a couple of doctors here in FatLand and told them about it. They didn't even know. They were astonished. When they looked at the site, they started to understand."

"So what did they do?"

"The first thing they did was to remove the electrodes from my brain. They warned me there might be consequences because they'd been in there for a while. But the only thing that happened was that I got headaches for a couple of weeks. Those disappeared, too."

"Did you start to feel differently about the forbidden foods?"

"Nah. I mean, I didn't feel sick anymore when I looked at them. I just wasn't tempted. Who knows? Maybe one day I'll try potato chips. I like other salty things." He looked at me. We both laughed.

"Good thing they didn't hypnotize you against that," I joked.

"If they could have, they would have."

"I sometimes wonder if Stark was leading up to that."

"Getting fat people not to have sex?"

"Maybe." He took a handful of nuts from the basket I offered. "Do you know that the doctors who helped me were just about to go public and institute an inquiry on behalf of FatLanders when—guess what. The site disappeared. Then we tried to locate the doctors who wrote the paper. Couldn't."

"Stark wanted to keep it from becoming public."

"He's already trying it again."

"What?"

Jimmy took a long sip of coffee. "He's targeting more foods. And people are getting three electrodes, not two."

"It's like a weight loss surgery of the mind."

"Exactly."

# 2045

**WHEN DASH DIDN'T GET BACK BY NINE** that night, Roberta and Janine became somewhat concerned.

"I'm going to try his smartphone." Janine clicked the key for one-number contact.

She said into the speaker, "What's going on? We're a little worried back here."

"That was productive," Roberta said.

**"MAYBE** he ran into a friend," Janine said.

"In the Safe House zone?"

"You never know."

**ROBERTA SAID** to Janine, "Go to sleep." It was 3 a.m.

"I can't."

"What good will you do anyone by falling off your feet?"

"If you say so." She lay down on the couch in Roberta's living room.

Roberta put a blanket over her and sat down in the old-fashioned rocking chair inherited from her grandmother.

After a few minutes, both of them fell asleep.

# Angela

**I WAS JUST ABOUT TO ASK JIMMY** about the other FatLanders who had had the same treatment with the Ceres Piper Project when my smartphone beeped at me with a message. "Your bags are packed. A taxi will be arriving momentarily."

"Jimmy is here," I said.

"I know. I just didn't want you bringing Margaret into this."

"What makes you think I won't tell her anyway?"

"Because you wouldn't want Jimmy exposed now, would you?"

"What do you mean?"

"He was very helpful to me during that nasty little reality show of yours."

*"Living Fat and Happy?"*

"He kept me up to date."

"Are you saying that he was an agent of yours from the beginning?"

"If the shoe fits, Angie. Have a wonderful flight."

# 2045

**THE ALARM WOKE THEM AT EIGHT.**

A message beeped on Roberta's smartphone. "Oh Lord," she said, her voice still thick with sleep.

"What?" Janine asked, her voice also sleepy.

Roberta sighed. "Okay," she said. "I guess you had to know sooner or later." She texted something, then said, "Dash is trapped in the wall mechanism. It basically holds an intruder fast so he can't escape."

"How did he get into that?"

"Hell if I know."

"What happens now?"

"The board has asked me to get him out without anyone knowing. The Safe House Security Detail and guards will look the other way. But it has to be done without setting off any alarms."

"Why did they ask you? Can't they do it themselves?"

Roberta looked at Janine.

"You're FIN, aren't you?" Janine said.

The comment coaxed a small smile from Roberta. "Are you surprised?"

"No, I guess not. But why would the board send you with us?"

"I am a certified and degreed archivist with a thorough knowledge of FatLand history."

"The board knows you're FIN?"

"What do you think?"

"You used to walk this?" Janine asked as they alighted from the rail service and whisked down the smart stair.

"Sure. It was fun. Through the woods and stuff."

"Part of the game?"

"Of course."

Roberta indicated the Safe House Gate. "See that?" she said. "That's where visitors present their permits, IDs and letters."

"We're not going there, are we?"

"No."

As they walked along the road paralleling the gate's perimeter, Janine said, "When was FIN created?"

"In the early days," Roberta said, "FIN's objective was to help people escape from the Other Side into FatLand."

"Why would they need to escape?" Janine asked. "I mean, wasn't the USA glad to get rid of them?"

"That was the strange thing," Roberta said. "You'd think that would be the case. But it was actually the opposite. The borders were the worst. We worked with people on the Other Side to get them through."

"I guess the USA was embarrassed. Losing face."

"Stark's Fitness Consortium was losing face. They didn't want it getting out how destructive the Health and Diet Laws were."

As they rounded the last square of sidewalk, Janine saw a gate and a very high fence with electrified wire running across the top. On both sides of the gate were two walls of the same height as the fence, but with only a few feet between them."

There, against the gate and hemmed in by the walls, stood Dash.

When he saw them, he looked up. Immediately Roberta put a finger to her lips and motioned that they were coming across.

She sat down in front of the fence and put de-electrifier oil on some rags she had carried with her for this purpose. After inserting the rags between the wires and the bottom spaces of the fence, she wrapped the cutter in cotton and more rags.

She cut two of the bottom wires and cut more rags with the scissors she had brought. She cut more wires on the bottom of the fence.

She latched a rope to the two bottom wires. Pulling on the rope, she pushed upward.

A section about three feet high lifted. Holding the rope, she gestured to Dash to lie down. She bound his hands and feet in cotton and rags soaked in de-electrifier oil. She gestured that he should move very slowly through the space she had cut and cleared.

Janine held her breath as Dash inched his way through. As he came through, Roberta gestured again for silence.

She removed the rope from the fence wires. Wrapping one hand in oiled rags and cotton, she pushed down the section of fence she had lifted. She reattached the slightly shortened wires to the posts on the ground from which she had cut them.

Removing the cotton and rags from her hands, she gestured for silence again and curled her hand in a "follow me" motion.

WHEN THEY were about two blocks away, Roberta took out the towel. She spread it on the short and uneven grass on the edge of the forest. "Lie down," she said to Dash.

Dash sighed in satisfaction as Roberta applied a disinfectant wash and probiotic cream to his fingers and parts of his hands and arms. She bandaged his bruises.

"You'll be okay," she said. "Start working your legs up and down."

He did.

Janine, who had been quiet up to this point, said, "I don't understand any of this. What set off the trigger for the walls?"

"An intruder sets them off," Roberta said.

"But I had my visitor's pass on," Dash pointed out.

"Which means that someone somewhere overrode a switch," Roberta said.

"They didn't want him to get out," Janine said.

DASH LOOKED at Roberta. "How did you know about all of this?"

Roberta said, "You may as well know. Janine figured it out. I'm FIN."

"What's that?" he asked, still working his legs.

"FatLand Intelligence Network."

"Is that why you knew someone might try to trap me?"

"Actually, they called me this morning because they knew you'd gotten trapped. They wanted to keep it quiet."

"Did something like that ever happen before?" Janine asked.

"They staged it in training," Roberta told them. "I took very careful notes. The Safe House Zone isn't the only place with this kind of setup."

"Dare we ask the other?"

"Classified."

When Dash was on his feet again, Roberta suggested that they take the walk back to her apartment in stages. "We'll rest a few times on the way." She drew out a flask and poured a capful. "Here," she said, handing the cap to Dash. "It'll help you feel better."

Upon reaching Roberta's apartment they put Dash on the couch and made sure he was comfortable. As they stood over him, asking if he needed more pillows or something to drink, he reached up to hug Janine.

*That's nice,* Roberta thought. *I do all the planning and work to get him out, and he hugs her.*

About three a.m. Roberta's smartphone rang. "Hello?" she said.

Nothing.

"Hello."

Nothing.

*Fine,* she thought. *Let's see what you try next.*

# 2045

**SMARTMAIL:** **TO:** **ROBERTA**

From: Vesta Myers

*I wanted you to see these before our next interview.*

"**AMAZING,**" Roberta said, clicking on image after image.

They sat in the courtyard of her building. In Alhambra and Art Nouveau style, there was a fountain with a mosaic floor around it. Colored lamps illuminated the water.

Dash leaned back in a settee. Janine leaned back in another, her hand on Dash's arm.

"What did she send?" Dash asked, his eyes closed, his face absorbing the sun.

"Paintings. Well, miniature images of them."

"Hers?" Janine asked.

"Yes. Remember she told us about them?"

"She mentioned them."

"They're all here."

"What's in them?" Dash asked lazily.

"Early scenes from FatLand. And they're—it's no picnic."

Dash pushed himself to sit up straight. "How so?"

"They show people digging. There's one of women getting water from a well. Someone else is showering from an outside faucet. Here's one of someone next to an old fan. Someone is pounding flour."

She handed the extendable smarttablet to Dash. He clicked on the images. "I see what you mean."

"How do we know she didn't just paint these out of her head for spite?" Janine asked.

"Make up scenes and paint them and pretend they're real?" Roberta asked.

"Why would she do that?" Dash asked.

"Discredit the Territorial side," Janine said. "Show that a state was necessary."

Dash said, "The convention voted for territory status."

Roberta said, "They didn't want to risk being part of the USA and having to enforce any part of the Health and Diet Laws."

"I think that is what carried it for them, in the end," Dash agreed. "But if these paintings were done from real scenes, you can sort of see why Vesta was making the case for statehood. They needed roads, electricity, water, sewers, like yesterday."

"But they—we—got all those things," Roberta said. "It just took a little longer."

"A little longer when you don't have indoor plumbing seems quite long," Dash said. "It reminds me of the way some of the villages near my home town looked. In pictures. About seventy years ago."

"So this was part of her push for statehood," Janine said.

Roberta said, "Did you track down any other people from that house, from those early days?"

"One," Dash said. He clicked and looked at the screen. "Marty Stevens."

"Where is he now?"

"North FatLand."

"We'll go to my place for that," Janine said.

# 2045

**THE HILL SMELLED OF PINE, COLUMBINE** and aspen. "If I lived here, I would spend my days sniffing the air," Dash said, taking deep breaths as he held Janine's hand.

His smartphone beeped. He didn't answer. Then a voice both mellow and sultry by turns murmured, "Miss you, lover. When you coming round again, honeycheeks?"

"'Honeycheeks'?" Roberta asked.

Janine removed her hand.

**"LISTEN,"** Roberta said about half an hour later. "I'm more than willing to interview Marty by myself. You two take some time to get things settled between you."

"They'll never be settled," Janine intoned, her blue eyes still.

Roberta sighed. "Then come with me. We'll go for drinks after."

"Yes," Janine agreed.

"I'll make arrangements for accommodation," Dash said.

"With lovergirl?" Janine sneered.

"That is neither appropriate nor possible," Dash said.

"Oh, really," Janine grumbled. "Then you might as well stay here."

"I don't think so," Dash said.

"Suit yourself," Janine said.

"I intend to."

"Come in," Marty Stevens said to Roberta and Janine.

They entered through a long, low porch. The house, too, was long, one-storied, with low ceilings. Roberta looked up, slightly anxious, but her head didn't bump.

"Have you ever heard of Frank Lloyd Wright?" Marty asked.

"Sounds slightly familiar," Roberta said. "Twentieth century. Architect?"

"You got it."

"You, too?"

"That's right."

"Oh, wait," Janine said. "You're the one responsible for a lot of the early architectural planning in FatLand, aren't you?"

Marty grinned. "Guilty."

"So you remember, then, when a lot of the first FatLand housing went up?" Roberta asked.

"I do, indeed."

"How long did it take before there was actual housing?" Roberta said. "I mean, as opposed to people living in tents and makeshift buildings."

"Took a while," Marty said. "In some cases, more than a year."

"Why so long?" Janine asked.

"Took that long to get the materials and figure out how and where, and get the deeds, and start building."

"So the approval process took a while," Roberta said.

"It did," Marty said. "You have to remember that they also wanted to build carefully and responsibly. They had a great planning person. I forgot his name."

"Was it difficult for the people who waited?"

"Difficult? How?"

"Not having running water. Or electricity. Or heat."

"Aw, hell," Marty said. "Wasn't so bad. That was kind of fun. A lot of them were neo-hippies. They liked the tents. And when it got a bit cold, they sat around the fire and made s'mores and told stories. If it got real cold, they slept in the dining hall or one of the other eating places. Or in houses already built. Everyone was willing to pitch in and help. Kind of like the old frontier days of the nineteenth century."

"People didn't mind digging wells?" Janine asked.

"Not really," Marty said. "I helped with that a bit."

"But in some cases you said it was longer than a year," Roberta said.

"Still didn't mind. My former partner, Ed, was great at building fires and digging wells. Geez, I miss that old son-of-a-gun."

"What happened to him?" Janine asked.

"He tried to get his mom in, over the border," Marty said. "They caught both of them."

"So they never got out?" Janine asked.

"The FatAndProud people managed to get them to Canada," Marty said. "I figured they'd come here after. But on the way, their first flight crashed."

"I'm so sorry," Janine said.

"Yeah, well," Marty said. "Been a while. Can I offer you both some coffee? Made some muffins yesterday, too."

"Sounds great," Roberta said. "Sure."


"DID YOU and Ed come to FatLand together?" Roberta asked as she sipped Marty's excellent coffee and took a bite of a blueberry muffin.

"We both came as part of a TV show," Marty said.

"TV show?" Roberta said, looking quickly at Janine. "Which one?"

"Oh, so you know about TV," Marty said. "Not many people do nowadays."

"A friend of ours specializes in twentieth century media history," Roberta explained.

"It was supposed to be a TV show," Marty said. "Somehow connected to the house. I never understood completely. But that didn't matter. I don't think it lasted very long, anyway. That's how I met Ed. They asked us if we'd like to live in the house and be filmed. It was free room and board, and they paid us for participating."

"How many people lived in the house?" Janine asked.

"Eight, as I recall," Marty said. "Kind of fun, once we got used to it. Also two other women, but not all the time. They were the producers."

"What happened after the show ended?" Janine asked.

"There was some messy stuff," Marty said. "I think one fell in love and left FatLand. The other—I'm not sure. Don't know what happened to her."

"HE WAS NICE," Janine said as they left with a basket of blueberry muffins.

"Yes, he was."

"Too bad he didn't know more about that TV show."

"He did know some things, though. Well, Dash will talk to him about that next time." Roberta added, "Do you realize that we didn't even have to mention Vesta and the paintings?"

"Yes. He had a completely different take on it."

"That's why it's good to get other opinions," Roberta said. "You still up for drinks?"

"Yes. I know exactly the place."

"Lead me to it."

SWILL AND SWEETS had the interesting distinction of serving chocolates with certain drinks, and actually suggested snacks to go with different beverages and concoctions. The FatLand Freedom—a mix of rum, cherry juice, pineapple and bitters—came with honey cashews. Roberta ordered it. Janine went for a Brandy Alexander accompanied by chocolate-covered ice cream bites.

They both sat back and sipped and took bites of their snacks.

"Robbie," Janine said, "did the board send you with us because you were FIN?"

"Probably."

"So they knew there might be problems?"

"I think they've been on edge since the Amiyah killing."

"Oh, yes. The dancer."

"That's also why they wanted all vehicles outfitted with touch alarms."

"But I don't understand why they don't just go after Stark. They basically traced it to him."

'They have their reasons."

"Is that an FIN matter?"

"More of an economic matter, really."

Roberta looked in approval around the room. It was all dark wood paneling, brick, wood furniture, subdued lighting. Not crowded yet.

"I was going to say—" she started, then saw Janine's gaze traveling to a man sitting in back.

He was rather hot, she conceded. Tall, thick dark hair, dark eyes, mustache, big shoulders, black tee, jeans, black leather jacket. She saw that other women in the room were glancing his way, as well.

She debated as to whether she should switch from her loose blue pants and long-sleeved walking suit to one of the other alternatives encoded in her smartclothes. *Too obvious,* she thought, but out of the corner of her eye she saw Janine switching her top to a black stretch shape that emphasized her large round breasts.

*Oh well,* she thought. "Better move in quickly," she said to Janine. "Looks like—"

"Looks like what?"

The voice came from behind her. She turned. Dash stood there, eyes large and lit with anger.

"Well, well," she said. "Finished smartwebbing so soon?"

"Not soon enough, obviously," he said, his eyes drawn across the room to where Janine already sat, the back of her head and upper body barely visible in the low light against the dark wood table.

"Aren't you being a bit unfair?" she asked.

He said, "I want you and Janine to report to the FatLand North Hotel. Now."

"I'd be fine with that," she said. "But I don't think Janine would. Looks like she's a bit occupied at the moment."

"Why aren't you occupied?" he said, bitterness clipping his already crisp consonants. "Are FIN people not allowed?"

"Not when they're on duty," she said. "But I'm not on duty now. I'm just lazy."

"You seem awfully forgiving of Janine's present activities."

"Forgiving? What's there to forgive?"

"Her seeming attachment to me, for one thing."

"What's wrong with her being attached to you?"

"Nothing was wrong. Now it is."

"Why?"

"You're joking, right?"

"Why?"

"How can you sit there and not think anything is wrong with what she's doing?"

"I simply don't see anything wrong."

"She's putting the moves on another man, that's what's wrong."

"Like you put the moves on another woman."

"That's different."

"Oh, really. In which way?"

"It's natural for men to want to try new things."

"And people?"

"Yes, that too."

"And it's unnatural for women?"

"Women are satisfied with one man."

"In which universe?"

"In this one. Many people have written about this."

"I think you've been reading the wrong books."

"So there are a lot of women who act this way?"

"As many women as men, I would say."

Dash clenched his fists. "Would you?"

"I don't know. Depends."

"Did you ever try to seduce another man when you were with someone else?"

'Not that I recall."

He said triumphantly, "You see?"

"I haven't taken a survey lately," she said. "But surely all men don't act the same way, either."

He gazed across the room. "Are you coming back to the hotel?"

"Give me half a minute."


It was with astonishment that Roberta heard a series of knocks at the room door only about fifteen minutes after she and Dash had come in. "It's me," Janine said, just short of yelling.

Dash clicked the "open" button.

"Hey," Roberta said.

"Hey," Janine said.

"I thought you—"Roberta stopped as Janine waltzed over to Dash.

"For your information," she said, "I did not pursue the hookup. However, I think you understand now why I was somewhat offended when you decided to sleep with someone else."

"I do," Dash said. "I wish I didn't, but I do."

Janine put out her hand. Dash took it.

"Come here," he said. "I don't know if we're in the mood for this, but I have to show both of you." He clicked for the dropdown screen that projected from the wall. Clicking again, he brought up a page of images entitled "TV show dedicated to happy fatties to air starting August 27, 2010."

"It's all here," he said. "These are the links. We can—"

The hotel shook. Explosions ripped through the room and terrace.

"Dash," Janine whispered.

**DASH LAY** on the floor, his forehead bleeding. There were shards of glass all around him.

Roberta and Janine called Emergency Services. No answer.

"I'm going to call FatLand Emergency," Janine said.

**FATLAND EMERGENCY SERVICES** ordered them to stay in the room, if at all possible, until they arrived.

"We don't even know if you can land here," Roberta said. "We don't know if there will be more explosions. Our fellow archivist is hurt and bleeding and unconscious."

"We can hover," FatLand Emergency said. "We can probably take you all right out."

"How long?" Roberta asked.

"Thirty minutes. Keep your friend covered. And watch out for the glass."

**THIRTY MINUTES** later they heard a loud whirring outside their hotel window.

"We're going to bust the second window," the FatLand captain told Roberta over her smartphone. "FatLand will reimburse the hotel if necessary. Please stand back."

Roberta and Janine watched as LG—the initials on her protective gear—shattered the window with a laser gun.

The helicopter hovered, staying right outside the window. LG ordered the medtechs in. They brought Dash out on a stretcher, put him into the helicopter and started to work on him.

"We're going to give you checkup exams," LG told Roberta and Janine. Just to see that you're okay. Nothing too long. Step in slowly. Take your time."

# Angela

I WAS JUST TOLD VIA SCRAMBLED SMARTPHONE message of a rather suspicious incident.

Dave now lives in Greece and is FatLand's Mission General there—I am rather proud of him. He and Esther keep up to date with everything in FatLand, and he keeps me informed. He was even good enough to tell me when Paul died. He said, "Stark said natural causes." I couldn't call Stark to check, but I can't think of a reason that Stark would lie about it. Even now.

One day the whole world will know about Paul. Or at least all of FatLand.

Dave just let me know that the room shared by three FatLand archivists was bombed. One of them was seriously injured.

I am gathering the notes I scribbled in various places and pieces. I will put them in order.

FatLand Archives and Historical Institute, meet Angela.

I have been quiet too long.

# 2045

FOUR DAYS LATER BOTH JANINE AND ROBERTA were sleeping when Dash opened his eyes, looked around and said, "I'm hungry."

The nurse assistant assigned to him said, "How about some toast and tea to start with?"

"Fine," he said. "As a start."

Janine and Roberta opened their eyes. Roberta grinned and said, "Hey, welcome back." Janine started to cry.

Dash put out his hand. The wireless monitors were capturing all of his stats—which, the nurse assistant declared, were looking just fine. Janine grabbed his hand and held it.

The nurse assistant returned with tea and toast for Dash and some tea for Janine and Roberta. They all thanked him and started to sip.

"Well," Dash said, sipping thirstily, "that was pretty weird."

"You're very lucky," the nurse assistant said. "Most people who have rooms explode and ceilings fall on them don't come out of it as well as you did. There was some swelling around the area of concussion, but the meds reduced it and it doesn't seem to be coming back. The bleeding stopped. The bruises are mending. If I were you, I'd go someplace far away."

"I think that's a good idea," Roberta agreed. "I've been in touch with the board, and they all seem to think we should go someplace for a vacation."

"Someplace where we're safe," Janine said.

*No such place, considering who it was and why,* Roberta thought.

*Stark knew we were on the verge of figuring out the link between FatLand and that TV show. He obviously had something to do with it that he didn't want revealed.*

She would have to be more vigilant and on her guard when they left.

# FatLand
## 2045

## Joint Meeting of the FatLand Board
### and the FatLand Archival and Historical Board

"**We are privileged to have with us today** the three archivists who have dug tirelessly, at great personal risk to themselves, into the holdings of various sites, and have gone to great lengths to obtain interviews and information pertaining to FatLand's origins. Their assignment was to find and search out papers, diaries, records, and recollections. They will now reward us with a summary of their findings.

"Please welcome Dash Sen Gupta, Roberta Held and Janine Storrs."

Dash began.

"Members of the board, members of the Archival and Historical Board, Archives staff, other proud FatLanders:

"Six months ago I was privileged to be appointed head of the Fat-Land Archival Exploratory Team. Sitting right next to me, on either side, are my two teammates—Roberta and Janine.

"Our first explorations were based on legacy materials, what we then hypothesized were 'takes'—the old term for recordings made during the preparation for the airing of TV shows. What we did at first is to confirm that they were indeed TV takes.

"Our next task was to try to ascertain what significance this show had for FatLand, if any.

"We delved into legacy sites about the show. Several of them actually disappeared during our research.

"We then conducted interviews and found out that the show was cancelled shortly after it started. What we have not been able to establish is the number of episodes that did air before it was cancelled, and why it was quashed.

"What we did manage to find out is that the show took place in the area that would become FatLand. So it continues to be extremely possible that the show had something to do with FatLand. We also found evidence of contact among FatLand and FatAndProud members in the very early stages of FatLand.

"Our research was indeed answering questions, but raising more. When exactly did FatLand become an official territory? Who were the people responsible? What kind of opposition did they face?

"We then proceeded to interview subjects who had some knowledge of these questions. We were on the way to compiling larger lists of possible subjects when the accident of which you are aware occurred.

"I won't go through the entire surveying process. That is in our written report. You will all receive copies and can read about this at your leisure.

"We ended up locating three boxes that contained folders of interest, some of which were directly related to the FatLand Territorial Convention, and some which contained other pertinent materials. We were able to establish that there was a 'first house' around which other houses then sprang up and were built, with settlements all around them.

"What we still wish to establish is what part that TV show played in building these houses, and why it was cancelled."

At this point a FatLand courier walked into the meeting room with a package in her hands. She handed it to the chair.

Reevie, present chair of the FatLand Board, removed the envelope from the top of the package. She took out a typed note and read aloud: "I think you will find that this memoir will be extremely useful in bridging many of the gaps you will encounter in historical records relating to FatLand. A Good Friend."

REEVIE HELD UP her hand for quiet. "I would prefer if our archivists opened this package." She motioned to them. "Please come up to the table."

Dash, Roberta and Janine stood up, walked to the table, and stopped in front of Reevie. She handed the wrapped package to them.

Roberta used a plastic cutter for the packaging. She extracted the typed manuscript, which was bound carefully in plasticite. She whispered something to Janine, who nodded.

"In view of the fact that Dash is the leader of this archival team, and especially in view of the fact that he endured serious bodily harm, we feel that he should be the one to open the manuscript and read the title page, if it has one."

Dash said, "Thank you." He took the manuscript and placed it carefully on the table in front of him.

"What I was going to say," he said, "is that we had in our hands evidence of several things in the folders: a link between the original house and the first FatLand settlements; a link between the house inhabitants and the FatLand Territorial Convention, and now, we hope, folders listing the votes for territory and statehood, as well as how a certain party tried to influence the vote. I cannot even tell you how excited we were, and then how devastated when our hotel was bombed. We remembered some of what was in the folders we examined, but there were other folders we had yet to look at closely. The shock and the loss we felt cannot be estimated.

"However, I can now see, just by looking at chapter headings, that the material we thought we'd lost is contained and corroborated here. And so much more."

A FatLand Archival Board member asked, "May we know the identity of the memoir writer?"

Dash thought for a moment. Then he said, "I am going to write it on my quickpod and pass it around."

Reevie quietly clicked in some information on her own smartphone. She said, "I don't want anyone leaving this area tonight. We are having sleeping furniture brought in. We are doubling the guards around this building. Our archival team believed that they would be safer here back in FatLand than anywhere else. I aim to prove them right. We will have meals and snacks brought in tonight and early tomorrow. Each of you will have an armed escort to one of our Safe Houses. The Safe Houses are under surveillance at all times. Your armed escort will be with or near you so that you are not trapped in any of the surveillance triggers by mistake.

"The person who has an interest in disrupting these proceedings has tried to prevent our archival team from exploring the origins and early history of FatLand. We must make sure he does not succeed."

"Is the memoir writer currently in FatLand?" a FatLand Board member asked.

Reevie keyed in a message to all the smartphones via the meeting network. The member who had asked looked astonished.

"Our archival team will secure the memoir in one of our archival vaults," Reevie announced. "Tonight it will be read by our archival team for as long as they wish. When they wish to stop reading, they will be accompanied by armed guard to the vault."

When Margaret saw the name of the memoir writer, she gasped. Reevie caught her eye in warning.

"For reasons that are probably evident, I will make the motion to adjourn this meeting," Reevie announced. "We will set a date for a continuation in a few days. Do I hear a second?"

"Second," a few of the attendees called.

"Point of order," a new FatLand Board member named Stephen called. "The chair has not read the rest of the agenda for the meeting."

"We will certainly read the entire agenda and more at the continuation meeting," Reevie said.

"I make a motion that in view of the exceptional circumstances in which this meeting took place, an adjournment should be carried out immediately,"Alvin said. He was Reevie's husband and a member of the FatLand Board, as well as the ranking member of the Medical Board.

"Seconded!" many members of the FatLand Board and the Archival Board called.

"The rules call for my motion to be voted on separately," Stephen insisted.

Alvin opened his mouth. Reevie shook her head and said, "So be it. We will have a vote on the motion. An exact record of the vote shall be made. The yeas and nays shall be recorded."

Each member declared a vote. The recording secretary then stood up and said, "The vote reads: One yea, twelve nays, one abstention."

Reevie nodded. "Thank you, Arkin. Since the vote is not in favor of the motion of having the rest of the minutes read at this time, we trust that the concern voiced by Stephen has been answered."

Silence. The attendees looked at each other, then around the room. Stephen was nowhere to be seen.

Reevie said, "This meeting is officially adjourned. Please do not leave the building. Dinner will be served shortly. There will then be more announcements."

She clicked a few numbers on the smartphone. Alvin walked back to where she sat.

"They have an all-points out on him," she said. "All the search protocols are in motion. He won't get far."

"After all this time," Alvin said. "He's still trying. And I don't mean Stephen."

"This is one battle he won't win," Reevie said. "This is our territory. He's not going to take it away from us."

Their hands met briefly over the table, touched, separated, then touched again.

"**Bloody amazing,**" Dash said a few hours later.

The three archivists sat around the table. They had all finished reading the memoir.

"Fills in a lot," Roberta said.

"It would be authenticated by an interview," Janine said.

"By message," Dash said. "She wouldn't have to travel."

"Best that way," Roberta agreed.

They all looked around. The guards stood near the door of the closed room.

"We could nail his hide with this," Dash said. He touched the bandage on his forehead. "We owe him."

"Do you think that's what she had in mind?" Roberta asked.

"We have to recommend," Janine said. "At least for the board to vote on."

# Angela
## 2045

**AFTER LONG AND CAREFUL THOUGHT,** I came to a decision.

Jimmy was astonished when he opened the door.

"I thought I'd never see you again," he said.

"This way I don't put FatLand in danger," I said.

"So I am your security, in essence."

"Yes."

"Like Moses. He was able to see it from afar, but he couldn't enter."

"Yes."

"You figure that it doesn't matter anymore?"

"Oh, it matters. But they have it by now."

"I know what I want to have," Jimmy said. He made sure the shades were drawn.

"Just like that? After all this time?"

"Just like that. You don't need your clothes, anyway."

I laughed. I whispered a short, ungodly prayer in my heart to Paul, or his essence. Then I stood up, turned down the light, and slowly unbuttoned the first three buttons of my sweater.

# FatLand

## 2045

"WE DO RECOMMEND TO THE FATLAND BOARD and the Fat-Land Archival and Historical Board that an interview be conducted to authenticate the information contained in the aforementioned memoir. If we are satisfied that the information contained therein is correct, we shall recommend further that Winston Stark be brought before the board and asked to answer for his crimes against FatLand.

"We recommend that the security measures taken to maintain the safety of the FatLand Board and the FatLand Archival and Historical Board shall remain in place any time the memoir is removed from the vault. We recommend further that a guard be put upon the vault for a period of two years. At the end of that time, the need for a guard shall be reevaluated."

MARGARET SAID to Ava, her crack reporter on the *FatLand Free Press,* "I was hoping she'd come back. I miss her. It's a great story."

"What are they going to do about Stark? He seems to have his fingers in every pie in FatLand. If they force him to disinvest, half of their funding for any new project goes down the drain."

"I'm not sure," Margaret said. "But at least they know."

"Kind of fascinating, that FatLand began because of a TV show," Ava said. "Strange, but fascinating."

"Very."

AFTER THE MEMOIR was transferred to the vault, Dash, Roberta and Janine repaired to the Safe House they had been assigned. There were now two guards at each of the three entrances.

"I want to soak and soak and soak in the hot tub," Dash said. "I want the water to invade all of my pores and take away all my stress."

"Sounds like a good idea," Roberta said. "You go right ahead."

"I didn't mean alone."

"I'm in," Janine said. She took off her jacket.

"Roberta?" Dash looked at her.

She looked away.

"Don't think, woman," Dash growled. "After all this time and all your training, can't you get it through your unyielding FatLand head that your wonderful, strong, soft fat body will be very happy in the hot tub with me looking at it from time to time and thinking what I want to do with it?"

"Um—" Roberta started.

"Um, nothing," Janine said. "Come on, Roberta. This way we get to tear off his clothes and play with him until he moans in ecstasy and begs for mercy."

"Well, if you put it that way—"

She followed Dash and Janine to the closed-off porch where the hot tub bubbled invitingly. Out of the corner of her eye, she noted the three guards stationed at each entrance.

*We have to keep winning our freedom over and over,* she thought. *My parents did. Now I do.*

*Then again,* she thought as she took off her clothes and climbed into the hot tub with less self-consciousness than she'd ever thought possible, *look at what we've already won.*

# Angela

**I AWOKE TO THE SOUND OF MY SMARTMESSAGER** beeping softly. Jimmy slept the sleep of the satisfactorily exhausted.

I clicked the smartmessager on and read the following: *Very astute, Angela dear. But you'd better watch it. I didn't come this far to have my business secrets revealed through a memoir.*

*Then perhaps you had better go further,* I typed.

*Don't tempt me.* The response was lightning quick.

*I don't have to,* I typed back. *You set your own traps. You always did.*

*The next one I set won't be for me.*

*Fine,* I said. *I'm going back to bed.*

*Say hello to Jimmy for me.*

*I will.*

I looked at Jimmy as he slept. I would have to leave his place soon so as not to endanger him. Especially if Stark meant for him to keep me here.

I smartmessaged a note to him and kissed the top of his head. Then I gathered my things once more and set out for FatLand.

# FatLand Time Line
## 2010—2019

SOME OF THESE EVENTS ARE REFERRED TO in *FatLand: The Early Days.* Some are alluded to in *FatLand.* Some will be referred to in *FatLand: To Live Fat and Free.* Others are mentioned here only.

2010    Recommendations from the Center for Health Matters note weight gain as a negative health outcome for pregnant women, with the implication that because many women between the ages of 18 and 50 are potential mothers, they are expected to adhere to the recommendations of the Center of Health Matters.

2010    TV show *Living Fat and Happy* airs. Cancelled after fifth episode.

2010    First migration from USA.

2012    First passage of Health and Diet Acts in USA.

2012    Second wave of migration from USA.

2012    FatLand named.

2012    Pre-territorial committee structure of FatLand set in place.

2012    Building and Deeds structure of FatLand set in place.

2012    FatLand internet structure created, set in place.

2012    First FatLand roads begun.

2012    First dining hall, restaurants of FatLand.

2012 FatLand Anthem composed.

2012 FatLand Medical Board created.

2012 First wave of home and office building in FatLand, largely financed by Winston Stark.

2012 First negotiations with USA on border protocols establish official crossing points with FatLand and patrols. Emigration from USA to FatLand is permitted.

2012 First FatLand Elementary School is created.

2013 First Fatland bars are opened.

2014 Second Passage of Health and Diet Acts in USA.

2014 First Re-Education Centers opened in USA.

2014 Third wave of migration from USA to FatLand.

2014 Land Apportionment Convention/Territorial-Statehood Convention held in FatLand.

2014 FatLand officially becomes the Territory of FatLand (June 21, 2014). FatLand Territory Day. FatLand Anthem sung for the first time. FatLand flag flown for the first time.

2014 The countries of Canada, Australia, U.K., Iceland, Belgium, Italy, Switzerland and the Netherlands recognize the territory of FatLand and send missions. The Territory of Samoa recognizes FatLand and sends a delegation.

2014 FatLand Constitution adopted.

2014 FatLand floats first bond drive.

2014 First FatLand complex of roads completed.

2014 FatLand Utilities Board meets for the first time.

2014 First FatLand newspapers and news services begin.

2014 FatAir airline created in FatLand.

2014 FatLand Transport service begins.

2014 Second round of negotiations with USA on emigration and border crossings takes place. Emigration from USA to FatLand is permitted for one more year.

2014    First Fatland Junior High School is built. First FatLand High School is built.

2015    Stark builds fortress in Colorado, USA.

2015    Legal emigration between USA and FatLand ceases. Negotiated agreement calls for short visits between FatLand and the USA only.

2015    The countries of France, Egypt, Romania, Israel, Tunisia, Mauretania, Greece, Turkey and Sweden recognize FatLand and send missions.

2015    Working with FatAndProud in the USA and in FatLand, FatAir airline expands and puts into place secret rescue protocols.

2016    The countries of Germany, Denmark, India, Algeria, Morocco, New Zealand and Mauritius recognize FatLand and send missions.

2016    First mortality statistics on FatLand compiled.

2017    FatLand coming-of-age ceremony for FatLand citizens is made official, with recommendation that the FatLand Anthem be sung at the close of each ceremony.

2017    The countries of Mexico, Portugal, Spain, Belize, Peru, Ecuador, Bolivia, Uruguay and Paraguay recognize FatLand and send missions.

2017    FatLand Athletics Board created.

2017    Block leader counseling system begins.

2018    First FatLand Writing Competition is held. Categories include novels, poetry, short fiction, plays and non-fiction. Winners are published by and in *FatLand Free Press*.

2018    First FatLand University is founded.

2018    A FatLand restaurant is written up in *Zagat* for the first time.

2018    First FatLand Arts Competition takes place.

2018    First FatLand Orchestra is formed.

2019   First FatLand catering hall is built.

2019   First FatLand Song Competition is held.

2019   First FatLand Varsity Teams are formed at two FatLand universities.

2019   First FatLand Village Clothing Coops are formed.

2019   First FatLand Debating Team is formed.

# FatLand Anthem
## (Tune: Fashioned in the Clay)

**WHEN A COUNTRY TOLD US** that we're too fat for their pride,
Tried to hold us down and made us feel so bad inside,
We all got together, figured out what we would do—
Spread a little love and hope to more than just the few.

*Chorus*
Fat and free, fat and free—
We are proud to live strong, fat and free
As we go through our full days living our lives
As sons and daughters, partners, husbands, wives.

Now we have a territory that we call our own.
Seven letters form a land that we have made our home.
F-A-T-L-A-N-D—we say this name and smile,
As long as we live here, we need never fear exile.

*Chorus*
Fat and free, fat and free—
We are proud to live strong, fat and free
As we go through our full days living our lives
As sons and daughters, partners, husbands, wives.

# FATLAND INCORPORATED AS TERRITORY
## June 21, 2014
## FatLand Free News

FOLLOWING A LAND APPORTIONMENT convention, the Territory of FatLand was officially incorporated on the first day of summer.

A festive and excited atmosphere greeted attendees and visitors to what was formerly a part of the midsection of the state of Colorado. A band played, dignitaries spoke, banners waved.

"We are beyond proud to declare FATLAND as a territory, and we welcome all fat people, as well as our thinner brothers and sisters, to this land of ours where people of all sizes need never fear ostracism or discrimination," the current chair of the FatLand Board, Dave Mesry, announced.

"For two years people have been pouring into this area seeking a refuge from persecution. The outflow of emigrants from the USA has tripled since the institution of the Re-Education Centers. We needed to become a territory to formalize our borders and provide the services that our citizens require. We hope to establish relations with all free states and countries.

"Meanwhile we now, for the first time, raise the flag of FatLand— our territory, our land, our home."

With these words the FatLand flag was unfurled and hoisted on a flagpole. It is purple, gold and green. The letters FATLAND are emblazoned on the bottom of the flag in gold.

Loud cheers rang out. The crowd then sang, for the very first time, the FatLand Anthem. Some were crying as they sang, but their smiles shone through their tears. People held hands as they sang and swayed.

The Constitution of FatLand, now being composed, will be read and officially declared at the end of this month.

# The Constitution of FatLand

**WE THE PEOPLE OF FATLAND,** in order to form a free and just state according to free and just principles, do ordain that the Territory of FatLand be open to those who accept that Fat People—people of heft, people of substance, people formerly styled "obese," people formerly derided as needing to lose weight, or "overweight"—are entitled to the same rights as those once accorded freely to those deemed to be of average size or thin.

We hereby decree the following:

There shall be no mention of weight made in any office, establishment or facility, public or private, commercial or nonprofit, in FatLand. Any person who breaks this rule shall be fined the sum of one hundred thousand dollars on the first offense, one million dollars for the second offense, and banished from FatLand for the third offense. Nor shall any health personnel be allowed to use scales to weigh patients at any time. There shall be no scales in any schools of any level in FatLand, including private and public schools of the pre-school, kindergarten, elementary, middle, high school, community college, technical college, and university/college levels.

There shall be no reference to level or division of weight or appearance in any establishment or facility or school or office in FatLand, public or private. There shall also be no reference to appearance of any kind, in any establishment or facility or school or office in FatLand, public or private.

There shall be no scales anywhere in FatLand, whether in establishments, facilities, schools, offices, or homes, public or private.

Any discrimination on the basis of weight, appearance, gender, sexual orientation, ethnicity, ethnic identification, religion, religious identification, or health in any establishment, office, facility, school, or hospital/medical facility, public or private, shall lead to a suspension of license of business or practice until and unless it is proven beyond a strong doubt to a Grand Jury that such discrimination did not occur.

All the costs incurred by citizens of FatLand in health facilities by citizens of FatLand shall be completely covered by the Health Insurance Policy provided by The FatLand Mutual Assurance Association.

Health care outside facilities for citizens of FatLand as determined necessary by medical personnel shall also be completely covered by the Health Insurance Policy provided by The FatLand Assurance Association.

No FatLander shall be required at any time to eat any food s/he does not wish to eat. No FatLander shall be prohibited or stopped from eating any food s/he wishes to eat, providing that such food has been inspected and adjudged free of pernicious bacteria and/or contaminants by the FatLand Health Board or their lawful representative(s).

No FatLander shall be required at any time to engage in exercise that s/he does not wish to.

A FatLander becomes a citizen upon residing in FatLand for two years if s/he has not broken any of the laws of FatLand and has not transgressed against the Constitution of FatLand in letter or in spirit.

No FatLander shall be made to travel to other states/countries/national entities if s/he does not wish to do so.

A FatLander wishing to be a member of the Board of FatLand shall have resided in FatLand for at least five years, shall have gained citizenship, and shall have evinced a clear and abiding interest in and concern for the welfare and happiness of FatLand and FatLanders. S/he shall be at least 25 years of age.

# On the FatLand Intelligence Network (FIN)

THE FATLAND INTELLIGENCE NETWORK was formed around the time that FatAndProud began working with FatAir to smuggle out endangered fat people from the USA, around 2015. FatLand Intelligence Network made sure that these efforts were kept secret.

FIN, as it came to be known, recruited in secret and kept its address and contact information secret as well. It did not wish Winston Stark to know of its existence. When it was revealed that Jimmy Carvie, one of its recruits, was a double agent also working for Stark, it made sure that Jimmy didn't learn that FIN knew of his dual allegiance. It also made sure that Jimmy did not reveal any of his knowledge of FIN to Stark.

Angela Barton knew about FIN and referred to it obliquely in her detailing of FatAir rescue operations. But she never named it.

Even though FIN was supposed to be a completely secret organization, it gained a reputation in FatLand for the extreme endurance and strength of its agents. The game Roberta's parents encouraged her to play, FatLand SpyClimb, was based directly on FIN training exercises.

# The First FatLand House

**THE HISTORICAL INSTITUTE AND ARCHIVES OF FATLAND**
have erected this plaque to commemorate and celebrate the first Fat-
Land house, purchased in 2010 for the TV show *Living Fat and Happy.*

The people who lived in this house at this time were:

VICKY WADE

KATHLEEN RENSON

VESTA MEYERS

MARTY STEVENS

ED GALLODIN

ESTHER SYLVAN

DAVE MESRY

JIMMY CARVIE

# About the Author

**FRANNIE ZELLMAN** received her MA in creative writing from Boston University in 1980 and blames none of her professors for what she has done or written since.

**SHE IS A MEMBER** of the National Association to Advance Fat Acceptance (NAAFA) and has taught writing workshops for people of size. She is the author of *FatLand,* Volume I of The FatLand Trilogy, and editor of *Fat Poets Speak: Voices of the Fat Poets' Society*, both also published by Pearlsong Press. She is currently working on the second Fat Poets' Society anthology and the third volume in The FatLand Trilogy, *FatLand: To Live Fat and Free.*

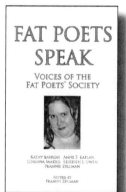

**SMART, SASSY, SENSUAL AND SOULFUL—** five women share the poetry and process of fat embodiment.

**WWW.PEARLSONG.COM/FATPOETSSPEAK.HTM**

# Volume 1 of the FatLand Trilogy

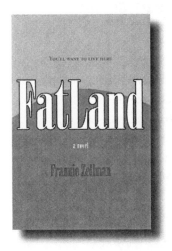

**In the near future** the Pro-Health Laws of the USA have become so oppressive that people seeking freedom over their bodies have established a new country. In FatLand, life is good and scales are forbidden. Free from the hatred and discrimination of the Other Side, FatLanders have built happy, productive lives. But not everyone is flourishing.

**Ava** came to FatLand after her lover died from bariatric surgery. She threw herself into work, believing she was immune from love. Then she saw a beautiful dancer and lost her heart again.

**Alvin and Reevie** thought that by living in FatLand they could give their children and each other a chance for a life free of sizeism and racism. They didn't count on their lovely twin daughters' curiosity and yearning for excitement and danger.

**Joann and Ed** carved out what they thought was a peaceful existence. But their bright children are anything but happy in the well-appointed home and tranquil life their parents had created in FatLand.

**Dara and Sandor** thought they could make the FatLand Board dance to whatever tune they wished. But their way of life and beliefs are about to be tested more severely than either of them could have imagined.

**Margaret** fled to FatLand after her rich, powerful paramour married a thin woman he didn't care for. She made a deal with her devil so she could publish the top flight newspaper FatLand badly needed. But then the devil called in the cards.

**Soon these FatLanders** and the remaining freedom fighters on the Other Side will face forces threatening the health and happiness of all.

**www.pearlsong.com/fatland.htm**

# About Pearlsong Press

PEARLSONG PRESS IS AN INDEPENDENT publishing company dedicated to providing books and resources that entertain while expanding perspectives on the self and the world. The company was founded by Peggy Elam, Ph.D., a psychologist and journalist, in 2003.

We encourage you to enjoy other Pearlsong Press books, which you can purchase at www.pearlsong.com or your favorite bookstore. Keep up with us through our blog at www.pearlsongpress.com.

## Fiction

*Judith*—an historical novel by Leslie Moïse
*Fatropolis*—a paranormal adventure by Tracey L. Thompson
*The Falstaff Vampire Files, Bride of the Living Dead, Larger Than Death, Large Target, At Large & A Ton of Trouble*—paranormal adventure, romantic comedy & Josephine Fuller mysteries by Lynne Murray
*The Season of Lost Children*—a novel by Karen Blomain
*Fallen Embers & Blowing Embers*—Books 1 & 2 of The Embers Series, paranormal romance by Lauri J Owen
*The Fat Lady Sings*—a young adult novel by Charlie Lovett
*Syd Arthur*—a novel by Ellen Frankel
*Measure By Measure*—a romantic romp with the fabulously fat by Rebecca Fox & William Sherman
*FatLand*—a visionary novel by Frannie Zellman
*The Program*—a suspense novel by Charlie Lovett
*The Singing of Swans*—a novel about the Divine Feminine by Mary Saracino

## Romance Novels & Short Stories Featuring Big Beautiful Heroines

by Pat Ballard, the Queen of Rubenesque Romances:
*Dangerous Love* | *The Best Man* | *Abigail's Revenge* | *Dangerous Curves Ahead: Short Stories* | *Wanted: One Groom* | *Nobody's Perfect* | *His Brother's Child* | *A Worthy Heir*

by Rebecca Brock—*The Giving Season*
& by Judy Bagshaw—*Kiss me, Nate!* & *At Long Last, Love*

# Nonfiction

*Acceptable Prejudice? Fat, Rhetoric & Social Justice*
& *Talking Fat: Health vs. Persuasion in the War on Our Bodies*
by Lonie McMichael, Ph.D.
*Hiking the Pack Line: Moving from Grief to a Joyful Life*
by Bonnie Shapbell
*A Life Interrupted: Living with Brain Injury*—
poetry by Louise Mathewson
*ExtraOrdinary: An End of Life Story Without End*—
memoir by Michele Tamaren & Michael Wittner
*Love is the Thread: A Knitting Friendship* by Leslie Moïse, Ph.D.
*Fat Poets Speak: Voices of the Fat Poets' Society*—Frannie Zellman, Ed.
*Ten Steps to Loving Your Body (No Matter What Size You Are)*
by Pat Ballard
*Beyond Measure: A Memoir About Short Stature & Inner Growth*
by Ellen Frankel
*Taking Up Space: How Eating Well & Exercising Regularly Changed
My Life* by Pattie Thomas, Ph.D. with Carl Wilkerson, M.B.A.
(foreword by Paul Campos, author of *The Obesity Myth*)
*Off Kilter: A Woman's Journey to Peace with Scoliosis, Her Mother &
Her Polish Heritage*—a memoir by Linda C. Wisniewski
*Unconventional Means: The Dream Down Under*—
a spiritual travelogue by Anne Richardson Williams
*Splendid Seniors: Great Lives, Great Deeds*—
inspirational biographies by Jack Adler

## Healing the World One Book at a Time